W9-BWQ-628

05/2020

THE
MISTRESS OF
ILLUSIONS

THE
MISTRESS OF
ILLUSIONS

BOOK TWO OF THE
DREAMSCAPE TRILOGY

MIKE RESNICK

DAW BOOKS, INC.

DONALD A. WOLLHEIM, FOUNDER
1745 Broadway, New York, NY 10019
ELIZABETH R. WOLLHEIM
SHEILA E. GILBERT
PUBLISHERS
www.dawbooks.com

First Printing, April 2020
1 2 3 4 5 6 7 8 9

To Carol, as always.

And to Jean Rabe—
writer, editor, horse-racing fan

THE
MISTRESS OF
ILLUSIONS

1

It has been a hell of a month, thought Eddie Raven as he walked aimlessly through a light rain in Midtown Manhattan. He looked at all the people walking past him, each in a hurry, no one paying him any attention. He simply sighed and shook his head. *If I told anyone what I'd been through,* he thought, *what has happened, they'd lock me away in the nearest funny farm and throw away the key—and I can't say I'd blame them.*

He grimaced. *I've been a Bogart clone in a World War II bar in Casablanca. I've been a Munchkin in Oz. I've been Mordred in Camelot. I've fought magicians and monsters, and I've been threatened or attacked with guns, magic, swords, dragons, and half a dozen other things. I've fallen in love a few times with different manifestations of the same woman, and I'm spending half my waking hours in a cheap one-room Manhattan apartment nursemaiding a badly wounded creature who bears very little resemblance to a human being and who seems to be the only one who knows all the answers to my situation.*

He decided to check on the creature, so he entered the building, climbed the rickety stairs, and opened the door to the tiny room. The occupant, who was totally devoid of hair, within an inch or two of seven feet tall, muscled like a weight-lifter, lying on a cheap cot, and making a rasping sound as he breathed, opened his eyes as Raven approached.

"How're you doing?" asked Raven.

I'll survive, came the answer. It did not come from the creature's lips, which did not in fact produce a sound, but the words were absolutely clear inside Raven's head.

"Is there anything I can get you?" asked Raven.

No.

Just as well, thought Raven. *What does one get a creature who looks like he escaped from a child's worst nightmare?*

"I've got to leave in a few minutes," said Raven. "I haven't seen Lisa since the shooting. She's still in the hospital, which is where you should be as well."

A grim smile played across the creature's lips. *Do you really think any hospital would admit me?*

"That's what hospitals do," said Raven without much conviction. "They admit men and women who need medical attention."

Well, there you have it, answered the creature.

"I don't know what the hell I have, except a girlfriend in isolation and a lot of unanswered questions," said Raven grimly.

They will be answered in the fullness of time.

"Spare me your bullshit answers!" snapped Raven, walking to the door. "I'll be back in an hour or two, and you'd better be prepared to tell me what I want to know."

I'll be here, was the answer, followed by a grim, almost frightening chuckle. *Where would I go?*

Raven walked out the door, went down the stairs, and was

standing outside in a cold drizzle a moment later. He considered signaling for a cab, but decided he was so annoyed that a walk in the rain just might cool him off before he was reunited, however briefly, with the woman he loved, the woman who—like the creature he had just left—had taken a bullet that he was sure had been meant for him.

He passed a plastic-shielded newspaper stand—they were an endangered species, but Manhattan still possessed a few—and looked at a headline. The Democrats still hated the Republicans, the Republicans still hated the Democrats, the Yankees still hated the Mets, the Mets still hated the Yankees, and everyone hated the mayor.

"Nothing's changed," muttered an unsurprised Raven, turning away and moving on.

He reached the hospital in another ten minutes, looked for a coatrack in the lobby, and of course couldn't find one. *Just as well*, he thought. *After all, this is Manhattan. At least this way I know I'll have a coat when it's time to go home.*

He walked up to the reception desk, only half trying not to drip on it.

"May I help you?" asked a middle-aged receptionist who looked pretty much the way he remembered his grandmother, only more harassed.

"Yeah," he said. "I'm here to see a patient." He gave her Lisa's name.

"Well, you certainly took long enough," said the receptionist harshly. "The poor thing hasn't had a visitor since she arrived here almost a month ago." She paused, glanced at her computer, and shrugged. "Probably just as well. She's only been awake for three days."

"I've been out of town," replied Raven. *Farther out than I think you can imagine.*

"Room 3435," she said, going back to her paperwork.

Raven looked around. "Do you have an elevator, or do I climb thirty-four floors?"

"Over there," she said, pointing to a door. Her expression said, *I wish it was you up there instead of that sweet girl.*

So, I'm sure, does the guy who shot her, thought Raven.

He walked over, hit the button, waited for the elevator to arrive and the door to slide open, and stepped inside. He took his coat off and hung it, still dripping, over his arm, then stepped back as two nurses entered at the twelfth floor and a doctor got on at the twenty-first.

Finally it stopped at his floor, the door slid open, and he emerged into a cluttered hallway that was filled with a number of trolleys bearing trays of food, drink, and medications. He checked the number of the nearest room, then began walking down the corridor until he came to 3435.

The door was half open, and he looked in. He'd expected Lisa to be tied to half a dozen tubes, probably with some breathing device hooked up to her face, but instead she just lay there, eyes closed, with no attachments of any kind, looking for all the world like she was taking a nap, which indeed she was.

He tiptoed over and looked down at her. There were no marks on her face or shoulders, and he concluded that the bullets must have hit lower. Her breathing seemed regular. Suddenly she tossed fitfully, and he gently laid a hand on her forehead.

She opened her eyes. It took them a moment to focus, but when they did, she smiled up at him.

"Hello, Eddie," she said softly. "I've been waiting for you."

"I'm just glad you're capable of waiting for anything at all," he replied. "How are you doing?"

"I'll be out of here in a few days."

"You were damned lucky," he said.

"We both were. I had a feeling that crazy man was shooting at *you*."

"He's had a lot of company since then," replied Raven grimly.

"I know," said Lisa.

He frowned. "How could you know anything that's been happening? I gather you didn't even wake up until a couple of days ago."

"Somehow I know."

"You've been watching too many gangland TV series," said Raven with a smile.

"You weren't being hunted by gangsters," she said.

I've got to stop, thought Raven. *She's so weak that if I make her concentrate on anything at all, she could lapse into another coma.*

"Well, they were very unusual gangsters, anyway," he said with a smile, hoping to end the conversation.

"When you're ready to talk about it, let me know," she said. "I might be able to help."

"I'm here and I'm safe," replied Raven. "I could have used some help over the last few weeks, but I'm fine now."

"You'll need help again, Eddie," she said weakly, closing her eyes.

"Would you care to explain that statement?" said Raven.

But Lisa had drifted off to sleep.

He stared at her for a long moment, then heard someone walking past the room. He stuck his head out, saw a nurse a few feet away, and called to her.

"Yes, sir?" she asked, turning and approaching him.

"I was talking to *her*," he said, gesturing toward Lisa, "and she passed out. I want to make sure she's okay."

"She's more than okay," replied the nurse. "She should have been dead—and failing that, she should be comatose for months to come. She is a truly remarkable woman."

"But she's okay?" he persisted. "Well, not okay, obviously, but normal for her condition?"

"She's breathing rather laboriously," said the nurse. "Everything beyond that is a plus." She paused. "Is she your wife?"

He shook his head. "Just a very good friend."

The nurse smiled. "Let me guess. Is your name Eddie?"

"Yes."

"I thought so. Every now and then she'd wake up long enough to yell things like 'Duck, Eddie!' or 'Don't trust him, Eddie!'" She stared at him. "I'd heard that you two were just innocent bystanders at some crazed shooting. She made it sound like you courted danger for a living."

He shook his head. "She must have been dreaming or hallucinating."

"Probably," agreed the nurse. "Along with what sounded like legitimate warnings, she also warned you against ogres and magicians."

"Did she name any of them?" asked Raven, trying not to show how interested he was in the answer.

"I don't think so. We were usually too busy calming and sedating her to pay much attention to what she said." She shook her head and smiled. "But I wouldn't be surprised to find that she'd seen *The Wizard of Oz* the same day she was shot."

"Oh?"

"Unless there's another film with Munchkins."

"Thank you for alleviating my fears," said Raven, who suddenly wanted to be alone with Lisa in case she woke up before he left the hospital. "I appreciate everything you and the staff here have done to keep her alive and point her toward recovery."

"She's *much* stronger than she looks," said the nurse. "I'm still amazed she lived through it."

"I'm harder to kill than you think," said Lisa's weary voice.

"Welcome back to the world," said the nurse. "I've got to get back to my duties. It was nice meeting you, Mister Eddie, and learning that there's someone who cares about her."

She turned and continued walking down the corridor, and Raven walked back into the room.

"You were listening," he said.

"To the part when I was awake," answered Lisa.

"Okay," he said. "What do you remember about Munchkins?"

"This is probably not the ideal time to discuss ancient movies," she said.

"Cut the crap," said Raven. "We both know what I'm talking about."

She simply stared at him, wincing in pain.

"You want to talk about seeking me out in Casablanca?" he continued.

"Eddie . . . please," she said weakly. "It's too soon. I can't . . ."

Her voice trailed off, and he realized that she was asleep—or unconscious.

"All right," he said, walking over and holding her hand in his. "I'll wait until you're stronger. But I didn't hallucinate, and I wasn't alone. I need to know what you remember, not only about the shooting but about everything that's happened since."

He learned over, planted a gentle kiss on her forehead, and left the room.

He walked to the elevator, took it down to the main floor, walked out into the street, and headed back to Rofocale's nondescript apartment, where he planned to insist upon some answers.

2

Rofocale was sitting up on the bed when he arrived.

"Don't you ever lock your door?" asked Raven.

"Eddie, it's eight or nine feet away," answered Rofocale. "I can't even walk that far." He paused and stared at Raven. "Did you see Lisa? How is she?"

"Alive."

"And?"

"And hiding something from me, just like you are," said Raven, making no attempt to hide his frustration. "And I'll be damned if I know why. Whatever I am or have been during the past few weeks, I'm sure as hell not the enemy."

"No one says that you are," replied Rofocale.

"Bullshit!" growled Raven. "Four-fifths of the people I've encountered in the past month think I am."

"That many people have been wrong before."

Raven glared at the creature. "Is someone paying you to avoid giving me answers, or do you just enjoy it?"

"Believe it or not, Eddie, I'm on your side."

"Against *who*?" demanded Raven.

"Against your enemies," said Rofocale.

"Damn it!" yelled Raven. "I didn't *have* any enemies until I walked into that idiotic fortune-teller's shop a few weeks ago. Then someone I'd never seen before killed the owner, shot you and Lisa, and got away before I could stop him, and nothing's made any sense since." He glared at Rofocale. "Now are you going to answer me or not?"

Rofocale's lips didn't move, but Raven could hear his voice, plain and clear, inside his head: *You have major obstacles to overcome before any answer would be meaningful to you, or even helpful. I'll guide you as best I can, for as long as I remain alive, but never forget that the fate of this and all other worlds depends on you.*

"What the hell are you talking about?" snapped Raven.

Just what I said. You are the most important man—the most important living entity—in the world. The galaxy. The universe.

Raven stared at Rofocale. "You don't *look* crazy. Fantastic, maybe, but not crazy—but you couldn't be any more irrational if you tried."

Believe me, Eddie, you are being sought and threatened by massive forces—massive and powerful. You don't know it yet, and I know the truth will be difficult for you to believe—but think back over the last few weeks and tell me if those constitute normal episodes in a normal life.

"Dreams," answered Raven with less certainty than he felt. "The shooting must have shocked me so much that I've been hallucinating."

Do you really believe that?

Raven considered his answer for a long moment. "No," he said at last. "No, I don't. For one thing, how could Lisa have had the same dreams?"

Good.

"But why are they after me—whoever *they* are?" asked Raven. "I'm nothing special. What possible threat could I present to them?"

You don't know it, Eddie, but you are very *special.*

Raven grimaced and shook his head. "There's been a mistake made somewhere along the way. I'm just plain old Eddie Raven."

The hint of a smile flashed briefly across Rofocale's face. *Rather than argue, let's try an experiment.*

Raven frowned. "What kind of experiment?" he asked cautiously.

Think back and tell me who your childhood friends were, what town you grew up in, and the name of your first love.

"What is this about?" demanded Raven.

Just do it, Eddie.

"What the hell," muttered Raven with a shrug. "If it'll make you happy . . ."

It will.

"Fine. My best friend was Skip Nelson, I grew up in Barrington, Illinois, and my first love—well, the first girl I was attracted to—was Marcia Barelli."

Very good, Eddie.

"Big deal. Now tell me what this is all about."

In just a moment.

"What next?" demanded Raven.

I've forgotten the names. Tell them to me again—your best friend, your home town, your first love.

Raven was about to answer, and suddenly nothing came out. He closed his eyes and concentrated. And frowned. And concentrated harder. And muttered an obscenity. Finally he opened his eyes and glared at Rofocale. "What the hell is going on here?" he demanded.

Your childhood memory is totally blank?

"You know it is," growled Raven.

Yes, I do.

"What have you done to me?"

Nothing recent.

"Explain!" yelled Raven.

Those were memories that were given to you, Eddie. On loan, so to speak. I have just returned them to their rightful owner, a man you will never meet, and who is completely unaware of your existence.

"Can you *do* that?" asked Raven.

Let's see. Please answer my question again.

Raven concentrated and frowned again. "I still can't."

You're sure?

Raven tried again and shook his head in bewilderment. "I have no past—or, rather, I can't remember one prior to the last few months."

I know.

"Explain," said Raven, trying to fight back the sense of panic that threatened to overwhelm him.

It will be difficult to assimilate, but you must try, Eddie.

"Just get on with it."

You were too powerful to kill in your true form, but your enemies were able to wipe out your memory, your very identity, and place your consciousness in another body—the body you now inhabit.

"Why?" demanded Raven.

Because they fear who you really are.

"Who I am?" growled Raven. "I sell wholesale suits and dresses in the Garment District, for Christ's sake!"

That is your disguise, Eddie. It was given to you—imposed on you, actually—once it became apparent that you were on their trail.

"Do you know how little sense this is making?" said Raven irritably.

How much more sense have the past few weeks made to you, Eddie? Believe me, you were given your physical appearance and your memories so that no one—and especially not you—would ever guess who you really are.

"And who is that?"

It is enough that you are their greatest enemy.

"*Whose* greatest enemy?" Raven all but bellowed.

Calm down, Eddie. Any further information could cause you to act in ways that are detrimental to our cause.

Raven stared at the creature on the cot. "What the hell *is* our cause?" he asked at last.

Everything will become clear in time. If you learn too soon, you will try to use your powers prematurely, with catastrophic results.

"*What* powers, goddammit?" yelled Raven.

Quiet, Eddie. No sense alerting them to your presence.

"Talking to you in your dingy apartment will alert some mysterious 'them' to my presence? Those bullets did you more damage than you think."

By now you must know better.

"I don't know anything," muttered Raven, reaching into his pocket for a cigarette and suddenly realizing that he didn't smoke. "I came here for answers. All I get is double-talk."

All will become clear in time.

"Screw it!" snapped Raven, getting angrily to his feet. "I quit. I'm going on strike until you tell me what the hell this is all about."

You *can quit, but* they *won't. You—and those who depend upon you—are in mortal danger.*

"I don't care," said Raven. "No answers from you, no cooperation from me."

You are our only hope, came the silent words, and the desperation Rofocale transmitted to Raven was almost palpable. *You must act!*

"Then tell me what I want to know," said Raven, standing by the door. "This is the last time I'm going to ask."

There was no answer, and Raven could see that the extended effort of communicating telepathically had robbed Rofocale of his remaining strength, and that he had lapsed into unconsciousness. Raven, who couldn't differentiate a faint from a coma, especially in a creature like this, decided to see if he could reestablish contact and peek inside Rofocale's mind, but all he got were nightmare images that drove him to the brink of madness before he was able to finally break the connection.

"Great!" he muttered as he walked out the door, down the stairs, and began wandering distractedly through the darkened streets. "The only two people who can help me figure out what's going on are both comatose!"

3

*O*kay, thought Raven as he stood on a corner, trying to ignore the drizzle that was rapidly becoming a heavy rainfall. *I've been a saloon keeper, a Munchkin, and a wizard. Maybe it's time I became something of my own choosing, something that can help me figure out what the hell is going on— always assuming that it is still* my *life.*

He closed his eyes, tensed his body, and waited.

Nothing happened.

Damn it! I've done it before, three times in fact. Now I've got to concentrate. Just how the hell did I do it?

He stood still and tried to picture himself as Humphrey Bogart in *The Maltese Falcon*. All that happened was that he got wetter and colder, and a cop began staring at him as if he might start tearing off his clothes or maybe pull a gun and begin shooting up the neighborhood.

He forced a smile at the cop.

"I'm okay, officer," he said. "Just working off a little too much to drink."

"Watch out for traffic," replied the cop in a friendly voice.

"I'm not that drunk," said Raven.

"I'll take your word for it—but if you stand that close to the curb, you're going to get drenched."

"Thanks," said Raven, moving across the sidewalk to stand under the protection of an awning.

"Take it easy, fella," said the cop, walking away.

Okay, thought Raven. *How did I do it?*

He tried to remember the circumstances of his transformations, and realized that *he* hadn't willed them at all. Casablanca—Bogart and Bergman's Casablanca—didn't exist, neither did Oz, and there was no reason to think he purposely willed himself back over the centuries and across the ocean to Camelot.

Then I didn't do it, he concluded. *They—whoever they are—did it to or for me.*

So he was at a dead end, three minutes after walking out of Rofocale's room.

And then it hit him: *Maybe not.*

He latched on to the thought. *I may not have chosen the destinations or the eras, but I was the one who was transported. That is my ability. I can move from here to—well, to* any*where. All I have to do is dope out how to steer through time and space and reality.*

He stopped and frowned. It *felt* right, but it seemed too crazy to be true.

After standing there for another five minutes without reaching any further conclusion, he realized that he was getting hungry. He looked down the block, saw six or seven establishments with their lights still on, and began walking toward them. The first five were bars, the sixth was a still-open magazine shop that wasn't even subtle about booking bets on the next day's races, and the seventh—the Golden Biscuit—was a diner.

He entered the diner, looked around for a table, found that the only three were in use, and sat down on a stool at the counter, where he ordered a cup of coffee and a grilled cheese sandwich.

"Still pouring?" asked the counterman.

"Yeah."

"Oh, well," said the counterman, "how much muddier can Belmont get than it already is?"

"You sure you shouldn't be working next door?" asked Raven with a smile.

"Nah," said the man, returning his smile. "If I stopped betting and went to work there, they'd go broke in a week."

Raven chuckled, and began sipping his coffee as the man went off to make his sandwich. When he returned he laid the plate down in front of Raven.

"Thanks," said Raven.

"My pleasure. Maybe we ain't as fancy as the Carnivore, that snazzy restaurant over on the next block, but who the hell wants hippo ham or crocodile steak anyway?"

"They really sell hippo and crocodile?"

The counterman nodded. "You wouldn't believe what they sell. If it's wild and not native to North America, it's on their menu—and if you live on Park Avenue or thereabouts, you can probably even afford it."

"Probably half the price goes to the guy who risked his life to kill what they're serving in the first place," suggested Raven.

"If it was me, I'd want ninety percent," said the counterman. "Hell, I get nightmares when my neighbor's cat hisses at me. I can't imagine what it feels like to stand there and face a charging lion."

I wonder what it does *feel like?*

And suddenly there he was, on the African veldt, staring down the barrel of his rifle as a huge dark-maned lion bore down upon him, roaring hideously.

This can't be happening, he thought—but then he remembered the very real pain he experienced in Oz and Camelot, and pulled the trigger as the lion was making his final leap. The huge cat fell dead at Raven's feet. His left forepaw twitched a few times, and then he was perfectly still.

"Well done, Bwana," said a voice next to him, and he turned to see a black face. The face belonged to a tall, lean man who reached out and took Raven's rifle away from him, and so was clearly his gun bearer.

Okay, thought Raven. *That helps narrow it down. He called me "Bwana," not "Baas," so we're in East Africa rather than South or southern Africa. But who am I, and what the hell am I doing here?*

He had no answer, and rather than head off in the wrong direction and walk into the jaws of the lion's companions or mate, he waited until his gun bearer started walking away and fell into step behind him.

They walked across the lush green veldt for perhaps a quarter mile, then came to a narrow river lined with acacia trees and began walking along it. In a few minutes a tented camp came into view, and a lovely auburn-haired woman waved at him. As he drew closer, he was able to make out her facial features. They were Lisa's.

Of course, he thought. *You've been everywhere else, so why not here too?*

"I heard the shot," she said as he approached her. "Did you get him?"

"Yes."

She nodded her head. "I assumed so, since there was no second shot. You are quite the marksman, Mr. Quatermain."

So I'm Alan Quatermain. And now let me hazard a guess as to your identity.

"Thank you, Elizabeth."

Just a pleasant smile, no other reaction at all. So you're Elizabeth Curtis, not Sir Henry Curtis, and that means we're in the movie, not the book—for whatever that's worth.

"You must be thirsty," she said. "Can I have one of the camp boys get you a drink?"

"I wouldn't say no," he replied. He walked over to a camp chair. "Mind if I sit down?"

"It's your camp, Mr. Quatermain," said the British noblewoman with Lisa's face and voice.

"True," he agreed. "But you're paying for it."

"I expect to be well-compensated when we find the mines," she replied.

"*If* we find them," said Raven.

"I have untold faith in your abilities, Mr. Quatermain."

"If you really mean that," he replied, "please start calling me Alan." *Oops! I almost said "Eddie."*

"Certainly, Alan," she replied. "Do you think we're getting close to them?"

Raven frowned. *Where the hell did Haggard put them? It's*

been a couple of decades since I read the damned book. "Difficult to say, ma'am."

"Elizabeth," she corrected him.

"Elizabeth," he amended. "The thing to remember is that finding them is only the first part of the problem. They figure to be very well protected. They could have hundreds of warriors guarding the place."

"Ah, but we've got *you*," she replied with a smile.

"I admire your confidence, Elizabeth," he said. "But I'd rather have forty or fifty armed men."

"No you wouldn't," she said.

"I wouldn't?"

"If you did, we'd have to split the treasure fifty ways, and I probably couldn't pay your salary out of what's left."

He chuckled. "I guess you're in luck after all," he said. "How much can it cost to bury one used-up old hunter?"

"Don't talk like that, even in jest," she said.

"I apologize, ma'am."

"Elizabeth."

"Elizabeth," he corrected.

She turned to one of the natives who were hovering around a small campfire. "I'll have a cup of tea, please."

The man gave her a snappy military salute, which looked rather ludicrous since he was wearing nothing but a loincloth and a colorful blanket, picked up a kettle, poured a cup of tea, and carried it over to her.

"Thank you, Njobo," she said.

He bowed, saluted again, and walked back over to the fire.

"Once again, Mr. Quatermain, how far do you think we are from the mines?"

"From the map's placement of the mines," he corrected her. "Let me see it once more, please?"

She instructed one of the camp attendants to bring her the ancient folded paper, not quite parchment, and handed it to him.

He studied it for a moment, then looked up. "It all depends, ma'am."

"Elizabeth," she said.

"I'm sorry. Elizabeth." He pointed to a spot on the map. "We're here," he said. "And we have to go"—he pointed to another spot—"*here.*" He paused for a moment. "Now, if this was a map of England, I'd say we could be there in two days without relying on public transportation. But of course, this is Africa, and there's not a sidewalk or a paved road within a couple hundred kilometers. And there are other factors. First, are there hostile tribes—or, just as bothersome, hostile animals—along the way? Second, is the map accurate?"

"I have been assured that it's authentic," she replied. "The paper, the ink, the—"

"I didn't ask if it was *authentic,*" replied Raven. "I asked if it was *accurate.*" He paused. "The map is hundreds of years old, possibly even a thousand. Is that correct?"

"Absolutely."

"Then clearly you are not its first owner. So how do we know that some prior owner hasn't used it and plundered King Solomon's Mines already?"

"You've been in Africa too long, Mr. Quatermain," she said.

"Trust me, if the mines have been found, no one could keep it a secret for a month, let alone a millennium."

"Let's hope you're right." She added, "And let's hope there are no surprises."

The biggest surprise I keep getting is meeting you in all these mythical places. You were charming as Dorothy, and captivating as Ilsa, and every inch a sorceress as Morgan le Fay—but I was never happier than when we were just Lisa and Eddie, meeting for meals, going on dates, and planning to spend the rest of our lives together. He grinned wryly. *Who'd have guessed that the rest of our lives included wizards, kings, magicians, Nazis, and man-eating lions?*

"You smiled," she noted. "Is something funny?"

"Probably I'm just happy the lion didn't eat either of us."

"You have a very strange sense of humor, Mr. Quatermain."

"Perhaps," he said. "But I persist in thinking it would be considerably less funny if the lion had won." He looked at the sky. "It's going to be dark soon, Lisa. Maybe we should have the camp boys start preparing dinner."

"Fine," she said. "And I'm Elizabeth." She stared at him. "Who is Lisa?"

"Beats me," he answered. "Sometimes I think I imagined her." *Hell, sometimes I think I'm imagining all of* this.

But you're not, said Rofocale's voice within his head.

Then what the hell am I doing here, a fictional character hunting for a probably fictional treasure, in a fictional version of a country I've never been to?

Just persevere, said Rofocale, *and all will become clear.*

You said that the last three times.

The thought that came through was hazy and garbled, and Raven knew Rofocale was losing consciousness again.

An hour later the camp crew had fixed dinner—steaks taken

from a Grant's gazelle he had slain earlier in the day—and he sat down on a canvas chair a few feet away from Elizabeth Curtis.

"It's very good," she said, indicating the steak.

"I prefer kudu," he replied, "but there's certainly nothing wrong with Grant's gazelle."

"So when should we reach the mines?" she asked, then added, "Assuming nothing distracts us."

"I'm more concerned about being attacked than distracted," replied Raven, forcing a smile. "The mines have existed for a millennium or two. *Someone* has got to be guarding or protecting them against intruders."

She gave an unconcerned shrug. "They're just guards. *You're* Alan Quatermain."

"But *they've* never read H. Rider Haggard," he replied.

She frowned. "Who?"

Oh, hell, of course you wouldn't know. You're living the story, not reading it.

"Nobody very important," he said with a shrug. "What do you plan to do with all the trillions we find?"

"First, of course, I'll pay off any debts Henry left when he died."

So you're single and available. That makes the risk almost worthwhile.

"And the rest?"

She shrugged. "I'm sure there are numerous charitable foundations that can use some economic help. And who knows? I may get married again someday. I don't want my future husband to be marrying a pauper."

"I'm sure he wouldn't care."

She stared at him. "Oh?"

"Just a hunch," he replied with a shrug.

There was a moment's silence, and then she spoke again. "You still haven't answered me."

"About what?"

"When we expect to reach the mines."

"I'd just be guessing. A lot of it depends on whether our information is accurate—and if it is, a lot more depends on who or what has successfully guarded them for a millennium or two."

"If you have serious doubts, you shouldn't have agreed to come," she said.

I don't remember agreeing. One minute I was in Manhattan, and the next I was facing a charging lion.

"The thrill of actually finding the mines makes it worth all the risks and uncertainties," he said aloud.

"Good," she replied. "Because there seems to be literally no one else with the necessary skills to lead this expedition."

I could mention Selous or Pretorius or even Trader Horn, but while they existed in my *world, who knows if they belong to this one as well?*

"I appreciate your confidence in me, Mrs. Curtis," said Raven.

"Elizabeth."

"I'm sorry—Elizabeth." He shrugged. "If nothing else, at least you'll get to see a lot of Africa."

"You make it seem romantic and beautiful," she replied, "but I know that it's red in tooth and claw. That lion you shot today was the third one to attack one of us . . . and then there was the elephant, and the rhinoceros, and . . ."

"We're intruding on their territory," he said. "They have every right to defend it."

"We're certainly not eating what the elephant and the rhinoceros ate."

He smiled. "They have limited intelligence. Hell, if they were smarter, they'd still rule this land, and such men as survived would be kept in cages in their equivalent of a local zoo."

She chuckled. "I like your imagination, Mr. Quatermain."

I like it a hell of a lot better than Rofocale's. What the hell am I doing here? In fact, now that I come to think of it, what are you doing here?

He frowned and stared at her for a long moment.

"Is something wrong, Mr. Quatermain?"

Might as well try.

"Call me Eddie," he said.

"You're Alan, not Eddie."

"Sorry," he said, forcing a smile. "That just slipped out. I had a friend who couldn't pronounce 'Alan' when I was a child, so he called me 'Eddie.'"

She stared at him as if he might begin foaming at the mouth any moment, then shrugged. "Actually, it's not a bad alternative. I think under other circumstances Eddie fits you as well or better."

"The trick is to find those other circumstances," he said, watching her intently for a reaction . . . but there was none.

Njobo brought them their coffee.

"Very acceptable," she said as Njobo retreated. "It would have been better with cream, but one can't have everything under these circumstances."

"Someday cream and sugar substitutes will be as common as coffee itself," said Raven.

"You say that like one who knows," she replied.

"I'm good at extrapolating," he said with a smile.

She returned his smile. "So you can predict something that will replace cream centuries from now, but you can't predict if and when we'll come to the mines."

I'd say "Touché," but you'd probably find that offensive.

"I could be wrong," he said.

"Let's just hope that the map and the information poor dear Henry collected about the mines aren't wrong." She stared at him. "What will you do with your share?"

"My share?" he repeated. "I'm just the hired help."

"If we find it, there'll be riches for everyone." Suddenly she grinned. "Which means, for you and me."

"I must confess that I haven't given it a moment's thought," answered Raven.

Which is why I keep wondering if we're even going to find them. Because a few handfuls of diamonds should have made me among the richest men in the world, but when I met you before all this began, I was just a normal guy with a normal income and normal debts.

"Well, that should give you something to dream about," she said, finishing her coffee and getting to her feet. "I'm going to retire to my tent and get some sleep. I keep hoping that to-morrow will be *the* day, and I'll need all my energy for it." She paused. "I just wish those monkeys would stop chattering."

"They're on our side," said Raven.

She frowned in puzzlement. "*Our* side?"

He nodded his head. "When they stop chattering, we'll

know that a lion or leopard is approaching the camp, and that we shouldn't leave our tents."

She smiled. "I never thought of that. Thank you, Alan."

"Sleep well, Elizabeth," he said.

She wandered over to her tent and entered it, and Raven found that he was carrying a pipe in his safari coat. He pulled it out and stared at it, and while he was doing so Njobo brought over a pouch of tobacco.

"No, thanks," said Raven. "I don't smoke."

"Then why . . . ?" Njobo frowned as his voice trailed off.

"Must have belonged to her husband," he said, and appreciated that Njobo had the courtesy not to ask what he was doing with it.

"I think we get there tomorrow, Bwana," said Njobo.

"I hope you're right," answered Raven. "We're not that far from the border, and I'd hate to go to all the trouble of getting more permissions."

"Then why bother?" asked Njobo.

Raven sighed. "No way around it. It's their country. They make the rules."

"*No!*" said Njobo harshly. "It is *our* country, and no one may tell us where we can and cannot go!"

"I knew I liked you the day we first met," said Raven with a smile. "But just the same, I hope we find the mines in the next day or two."

"So do I."

"What will you do with your money?" asked Raven.

"Easy," answered Njobo. "I will give it to a white farmer for a dozen cows. And then . . ." He smiled and sighed.

"And then?" prompted Raven.

"I will buy twelve young and beautiful brides."

"No wonder you come with me on every hunt and every trek," said Raven with a chuckle. "You're clearly building up your stamina."

Both men laughed.

Raven decided that as long as he was carrying a pipe he might as well try the damned thing, so he filled it, lit it, and tried to remember not to inhale.

"If you get twelve wives, you won't be able to come out on safari with me," he said.

"Certainly I will, Bwana," said Njobo.

Raven smiled. "I admire your notion of a happy home life."

"They will be too busy caring for my sons and daughters to miss me."

"Now why didn't *I* think of that?" said Raven with a chuckle.

"First, because you are a white man, and second, because you do not belong here."

"What makes you say that?" asked Raven sharply.

"You look like Alan Quatermain, and you shoot like Alan Quatermain," said Njobo. "But you do not speak or think like him."

"Then why have you stayed with me on this safari?"

"Because you are a good man, and the woman depends on you, and before long you're going to need all the help my men and I can give you."

"Why?" asked Raven promptly.

Njobo smiled. "If you were really Alan Quatermain you would have read the signs the last three days."

"What signs?" demanded Raven.

Njobo smiled. "You see?"

"What did the signs say?"

"Keep away."

"Just that?"

Njobo shook his head. "Keep away—or die."

That's damned good advice, Eddie, he said to himself. *Maybe you ought to take it, no matter how good a shot you are as Quatermain.*

"We will not tell the *memsaab*," said Raven at last.

"We work for you, Bwana—not for her," agreed Njobo.

"Okay. Point out the next couple of signs when we come to them."

"I will."

"Okay," said Raven, heading off to his tent. "Might as well get some sleep while I can."

"I have had two men guarding your tent every night while you sleep," said Njobo.

Raven was about to tell him not to bother. Then he thought about it, thanked Njobo, and entered his tent. He sat down on his cot, elbows on knees, fists propping up jaw, and considered the situation.

Hey, Rofocale—are you there?

No answer.

Okay, it just meant that he would have to use his combined skills as Raven and Quatermain to solve whatever problems Fate chose to throw at him next.

He wasn't sure, but he had a feeling that Fate was chuckling at the thought.

4

They were up bright and early, as usual—it seemed to Raven that no one ever slept late in Africa—then had a quick breakfast and hit the trail. Raven studied the map, wished some of the landmarks were familiar to him or that some of the words made more sense, then gave it to Njobo to hold (and, he hoped, to secretly read).

They disturbed a herd of impala that was grazing peacefully and suddenly thundered off in a panic, received a baleful glare from a leopard that had been stalking them in the high grass, and stopped when they came to a stream.

Njobo came over and said, in tones so low only Raven could hear, "We are getting near."

"Oh?"

Njobo nodded his head. "They are not far from this stream."

Raven frowned. "Are you sure? Everything looks the same—flat, green, unexceptional."

"What better place to remain hidden for all these eons?" replied Njobo with a smile.

Raven walked over to where Elizabeth was standing. "I think it'll be today," he said.

"How I wish I'd brought along a camera!" she said. "Just

to prove to people that we found the mines," she added with a smile.

"You start flashing a few hundred diamonds and they'll figure it out by themselves," replied Raven, returning her smile.

"You know, Mr. Quatermain, we haven't given a moment's thought as to how we're going to bring the spoils, such as they are, back with us."

"We've got Njobo and seven other men," said Raven. "Each one can easily carry enough to buy a small country or two."

She chuckled. "I like the way you think, Mr. Quatermain."

"And I like almost everything about you, Lisa," he replied.

"Elizabeth," she corrected him.

"I apologize, Elizabeth."

"I wonder about this Lisa," she said. "I get the feeling you were quite taken with her."

He sighed deeply. "Quite."

"What did she look like?"

"Look into a mirror," said Raven.

"I mean really."

"A bit like Morgan le Fay, a bit like Ingrid Bergman, even a little like a girl on her way to Oz."

"I don't understand any of the references," she said.

"Why should you?" he said, half wistfully and half bitterly. "After all, you're Elizabeth Curtis."

She stared at him. "Are you quite all right, Mr. Quatermain?"

He nodded his head. "Yeah, I suppose so. But I'd be even better if you'd start calling me Alan."

"That would be quite improper"—a sudden smile—"Alan."

"I won't tell anyone if you won't," he said.

She was about to reply when they heard trumpeting off to their left. He turned and held his binoculars up to his eyes.

"Is there a problem?" she asked.

He stared for another moment, then chuckled and lowered the binoculars. "A pair of outraged mothers."

She frowned. "Outraged mothers?"

"A pride of lions that's hunting wildebeest got a little too close to two or three elephant babies. The trumpeting was just to scare them off."

"Good!"

"I agree," he said. "Now if we could just scare off whoever or whatever's guarding the mines . . ."

"*Is* someone?" she asked.

"They wouldn't remain undiscovered if someone wasn't," he answered.

She sighed deeply. "Sometimes I wonder if it's worth the effort. It was Henry's dream, and he's gone now."

"So now it can be your dream," said Raven. "It certainly belonged to enough others over the centuries."

"Henry left me very well off," she replied. "I'm paying for this out of petty cash. As we get closer, I keep wondering how badly I want those diamonds."

Raven shook his head. "It's not the diamonds."

"It isn't?"

"It's how badly you want to be the first person to enter the mines, to be the first person to definitely find them after so many have failed."

She considered what he had said. "I suppose you're right. And why are *you* here, Mr. . . . Alan?"

"Because I'm not in Manhattan," he said bitterly.

"I beg your pardon?" she said. "Have you ever been in Manhattan?"

He shrugged. "There are days when I wonder," he replied.

"About what?"

"Don't get me started," he said with a bitter smile, "or we'll die of old age before we cover the last couple of miles." He looked ahead. "Might as well get moving. You never know who might be coming from a different direction."

He signaled to Njobo, who in turn signaled to his men, and soon the entire party was walking again, Raven constantly forcing himself to walk more slowly so that Elizabeth/Lisa didn't find herself trailing her entire party. Every half hour or so they had to chase an animal or two out of their path, but they proceeded without any serious incident until mid-afternoon.

"Why are we stopping, Mr. Quatermain? I mean, Alan?"

"If the map is right, it's just around that cluster of termite mounds by the hill there," replied Raven. "If it's protected, and the odds are that it is, I'd like to try to spot them before marching straight in."

"Sensible," she said, nodding her head. "Very sensible."

They stood where they were for a few minutes. Then Raven waved Njobo and two others ahead, pointing to where he wanted them to station themselves.

"Shouldn't we proceed?" she asked.

"As soon as they tell us to," replied Raven.

A moment later Njobo waved an arm.

"Now," said Raven, taking her by the arm and starting to walk forward.

They reached Njobo in another minute.

"So where are they?" asked Raven.

Njobo pointed to a spot just behind the termite mounds.

"Good!" Raven turned to Elizabeth/Lisa. "I hope you're tired of merely being a millionaire, because you're about to come into some really *big* money."

"I'll just have to adjust to it," she said with a smile. She took a step, then paused. "You're sure it's safe?"

"Njobo says it is, and I trust him."

"Then let's go."

They reached the first of the termite mounds. Raven smiled at her. "Two more steps and we're—"

The transition was swift, painless, almost instantaneous.

Oh, goddamnit! he tried to scream, but nothing came out— and then, suddenly, he found that he was sitting in a chair in his apartment.

Alone.

It took him a couple of minutes to realize that he really was back in Manhattan. Then he immediately left his apartment, walked out of the building, and went to the featureless building that held Rofocale's single room. He climbed the stairs, considered knocking, decided that Rofocale was in no shape to walk over and open the door (or lock it, when he had left previously), and just entered.

The large reddish entity, which Raven thought of alternately as a man and a creature, lay on the bed. In fact, it looked like he hadn't moved since Raven had last seen him.

"Rofocale?" he said softly.

There was no response.

"Goddamnit, I'd like some answers!"

Rofocale didn't move.

For a moment Raven thought he was dead, but then he saw his chest rise and fall and knew the man (or whatever) was still alive.

"Damn it!" growled Raven. "A few days ago, or a week, or a month, who the hell knows anymore, I was just a normal guy, taking my lady around town and figuring I'd propose to her that night, or at least by the weekend. Then we walk into that idiot fortune-teller's shop, the owner gets killed, you get shot, Lisa gets shot, and I spend the next—hours, days, weeks, who the hell knows—trying to get back here from Casablanca and Oz and Camelot and Africa. In the process I lose my memory of everything meaningful in my life—my past, my friends, my accomplishments if any—and here we are. You're still uncon-scious, and who the hell knows where Lisa is or even *who* she'll be next? What did I ever do to deserve this?"

It's not what you've done, said Rofocale's voice inside his head. *It's what you* can *do.*

"Am I some kind of threat?" demanded Raven. "And if so, to whom? And what has Lisa got to do with it?"

Questions, questions.

"Then how about some answers, answers, now that you're awake?"

That would be telling.

"You bet your ass it'd be telling!" snapped Raven. "And if you still want to be attached to your ass and other body parts by morning, you'd better start answering some questions."

I know it's hard for you to grasp, Eddie, but everything makes sense, even if you can't see it—and on the day you can *see it, you'll be able to put what you've learned to use.*

"Stop sounding like a quiz show for four-year-olds and just answer some simple questions," growled Raven. "Like why do I keep winding up in these other worlds?"

They are all your world, Eddie—or at least versions of it.

"All right, other realities, then. Why is Lisa in all of them? Why aren't you in any of them?"

Good questions, Eddie. I approve.

"A little less approving and a little more answering, damn it!" snapped Raven.

I wish I could do what you want, Eddie, but even I am bound by rules.

"By *what* rules?" demanded Raven.

By ... the ... most ... stringent ... kind.

Suddenly the mental connection weakened and faded, and Raven knew that Rofocale had passed out again. He decided to check the man/creature's wounds and determine whether to call 911 and have him carted back off to the hospital.

He walked over to the bed, pulled the covers back from Rofocale's torso, and stared, frowning. The hideously infected wound that had covered half his chest and was festering just a few days ago was completely healed. The shot to his belly was now no more than a scratch.

What the hell am I dealing with? he wondered—and then, given his experiences since the shooting, he decided that it was time to hunt for answers rather than wait for them to seek him out.

His mind made up, Eddie Raven walked out of the room, shut the door behind him, decided not to trust the dilapidated elevator, went down the stairs and out into the cool night air, clearly a man with a renewed sense of purpose.

He knew he didn't want to go back to his apartment, because he was sure all he would do was sit around and brood, and that wasn't going to solve his problem. The only place he had a key to was his office in the Garment District, and he turned and started walking there. He was only panhandled three times—a record—and within twenty minutes he unlocked the door, tried to ignore the stale air, turned on a light, and sat down at his desk.

Okay, I've been a saloon keeper, a Munchkin, a white hunter, even Mordred, so I guess I can be a detective too.

He frowned.

What would a shamus do? Well, first of all he'd collect clues to help solve his problem . . . but my clues are in Oz and Camelot and Africa, so what do I do instead?

He grimaced and frowned again.

I suppose the thing to do is start putting together a case for who I am and who my enemies are—and the place to start is right here in my world. Or at least what I think of as my world.

Now, I truly believe that I am Eddie Raven. I believed it when I was a Munchkin or a hunter, so maybe I should begin by making sure I'm right.

"And I'd damned well better be right!" he growled aloud. "If I'm not, then . . . hell . . . I don't know."

"I wish you wouldn't cuss quite so much," said a familiar voice. "You'll scare away all our clients."

"Where are you?" he demanded, looking around.

The door opened. "I was just getting some coffee."

He stared at her. It was Lisa, all right, but Lisa with a difference. She wore a short miniskirt, an exceptionally tight sweater, had a pen tucked behind her left ear, and carried a cup of coffee in her right hand.

"Lisa?" he said.

She sighed deeply. "Velma," she said. "It's Velma, Eddie."

He frowned. "You're Lisa, damn it!"

She shook her head. "Get real, Eddie! This is the Eddie Raven Agency," she replied. "Everyone knows that private eyes go around packed, wear trench coats, and have secretaries named Velma."

"What if I call you Lisa instead?"

"I'll spill my coffee on you and take that job Snake McDougal has been offering me," she said. "*He* knows how to treat a secretary."

He considered what she said for almost a full second, resisted the urge to suggest that McDougal's last secretary probably wound up in the room next to Lisa's in the hospital, and leaned back. "Pull up a chair, Velma."

"Thanks," she said, seating herself opposite him on the far side of the desk. She picked up a pad of paper, thumbed through it, nodded to herself, took the pen from behind her ear, and stared at him. "So what have we got so far?"

He grimaced. "Not much. What the hell was the name of the phony little mystic whose shop got shot up at the beginning of all this?"

Velma checked the notepad. "Mako."

"I suppose he's dead now?"

"Yes."

He sighed. "Yeah, it was too much to hope for. Any description of the shooter?"

She smiled grimly. "Seven eyewitnesses saw him fleeing— and there are seven different descriptions of him."

"Why am I not surprised?"

"Because you're a detective."

"Maybe I should have sold suits and dresses instead," he said. "At least we're in the right neighborhood."

"Eddie Raven selling three-piece suits and floor-length gowns?" she said. "Don't make me laugh."

"Wouldn't dream of it," he said. "Okay, so after the killer left, there were just four of us in the shop."

"Well, three plus a corpse."

"Right," said Raven. "And that's the puzzle."

Velma frowned. "I don't follow you, Eddie."

"Clearly the shooter wasn't there to kill Mako."

"Why not?" she asked. "It makes as much sense as anything."

Raven shook his head. "If Mako was his target, why stick around?"

"You're not thinking this through, Eddie," said Velma firmly. "He wasn't 'sticking around,' as you put it. He was killing witnesses."

"No," said Raven emphatically. "He never fired a shot at me."

"I hadn't thought of that," she admitted.

"And if he was good enough to put a single shot through Mako's eye, how did he manage to put a couple of bullets each into you and Rofocale when you were both defenseless, and fail to kill you as well?"

"Into me?" she said, frowning. "I wasn't there. And who is Rofocale?"

"The big guy who *was* there."

She sighed deeply. "I don't know the answer."

"So nobody seems to have gotten a look at him either?"

She shook her head.

"Okay, we'll just have to tackle it from a different angle."

"Sounds good to me, Eddie."

"What's become of the shop?" said Raven. "After all, if he wanted Lisa and Rofocale dead, he'd have put another bullet or two into each of them. I think he was just getting rid of witnesses, and that his real target was Mako. So what's happened to the store—and while we're at it, was anything missing?"

"You already told me to check that out," said Velma.

"I did?" he said, surprised.

She nodded. "And everything's still in the shop. I gather it's being auctioned off next month."

"And nothing's missing?"

"They don't think so." Suddenly she smiled and shrugged. "But given what was there—all those exotic trinkets—who the hell would know?"

"Lisa doesn't talk like that," he noted with a frown.

"I'm Velma, Eddie," she replied.

"Okay, point taken," said Raven. "So we come to the real mystery."

"Which is?"

"Nobody in that shop carried a weapon except the killer. So why did he shoot three of you and leave me alone?"

"Maybe he ran out of bullets," she suggested.

He grimaced and shook his head. "That's a Velma kind of answer. Be Lisa for a while and help me figure this out."

"I *am* Velma," she insisted.

"Okay," said Raven. He stared at the featureless wall off to his left. "This is gonna sound crazy, but I can only come up with one answer."

"That's one more than I've got," she replied. "What is it?"

"He has some purpose for me," said Raven. "I don't know what it is yet, but he *let* me live." He frowned. "Given this milieu, I wouldn't be surprised if he shows up one of these hours or days and thinks I *owe* him."

"You know, that makes sense," said Velma.

"Damn!" muttered Raven.

"What is it, Eddie?"

"I'm not really a part of this world, but *you* are," answered Raven. "And if you think it makes sense, then it almost certainly does." He wished he hadn't given up smoking. He felt like he'd kill for a bent Camel, which was strange since he'd never smoked a Camel in his life, and indeed hadn't had a cigarette since he was a teenager. But based on all the mystery novels he'd read, smoking bent Camels was just how cheap hardboiled detectives calmed their nerves. "So do I wait for him here, or do I walk outside and show myself—and if I do, does he still have some reason not to shoot me?"

"This sounds like it's going to be one of your tougher cases, Eddie," said Velma. "At least in the past couple of months, anyway."

"I've had tougher?" he asked.

"Of course."

"Such as?"

"How could you forget the Three-Legged Showgirl, or the Black-and-Blue Mailer?" said Velma. "Or the Balinese Pelican?"

"You know," said Raven, "if I survive this case, maybe I'll

pack it in and become a mystery writer. Sounds like I've got a lot of material to draw upon."

"Would you put me in one of your books—would you, Eddie?" said Velma eagerly.

"Sure," said Raven. *Hell,* he thought, *you're my source for them.* "But let's solve this one first. I'd hate to get to chapter fifteen and have that bastard shoot me right before I sit down to write the climax."

"Don't joke about it," she said. "You get shot at often enough as it is."

"Am I smiling?" he replied.

There was a brief pause.

"Well," said Raven, "I can either sit around here waiting for clients and a crazed shooter, or I can go out looking for clues."

"I vote for clues," said Velma.

"Oh?"

"Your clients all look like Playmates, and most of them are married to missing millionaires," she said. "I don't see how that can help us find the man we're looking for."

"A depressing but telling point," agreed Raven. He got to his feet, donned his shoulder holster after making sure the gun was loaded, then put on his loose-fitting jacket that he was sure hid the gun, even though Velma assured him that it didn't. "Okay," he said, walking to the door. "Let's go."

"Where?" she asked.

"The logical starting point is Mako's place, whatever the hell it's called."

"It's all boarded up, Eddie," she said.

"Still? The shooting was weeks ago."

"Still," she said. "I passed by it just yesterday."

"What the hell," said Raven. "It's still the logical place to start."

"But I told you: it's locked and boarded up."

"So what?" he said with a smile. "I'm a detective."

"I don't want you to get yourself killed, Eddie."

"We're in agreement on *that*, anyway," said Raven.

"There are other, safer ways to go about this," she said.

"But none of them are as fast," he replied, "and for all I know I'm being hunted by a nut case with a gun."

Velma sighed. "Okay, Eddie—let's knock him dead."

She opened the door and fell into step behind him as he walked out into the corridor.

They'd walked two blocks when Raven stopped, frowning.

"What is it, Eddie?" asked Velma.

"Something's wrong," he said. "Everyone's staring at me."

She smiled. "No, Eddie," she said. "They're staring at *me*. It happens all the time."

He turned to her. "I guess you're right."

She waited for a few seconds. "Now you're staring too."

"Damn," he muttered. "I apologize. Let's get moving."

They reached Fifth Avenue and turned north, then walked a few more blocks until they came to the shop.

"Amazing," said Raven.

"What is, Eddie?"

"It's still boarded up."

"I told you it was," said Velma.

"I know . . . but a location like this has to go for a few thousand a month. You'd think the owner would be screaming for them to open it up."

"Maybe he is," she said. "Would it make a difference?"

Raven shrugged. "No, probably not."

He approached the door, examined the locks—both the one that came with the building and the two the police had added, and then studied the boards that had been nailed over the windows.

"They were thorough," he said. "I'll give them that."

"Then we can't get in?" asked Velma.

"Of course we can get in," he replied. "I'm a shamus, remember? No lock can keep me out."

"Well, then?" she said as he stood there, staring into the shop through a small piece of uncovered window. "If no lock can keep you out . . ."

"Those aren't locks standing right across the street staring at us," answered Raven. "Those are uniformed cops. C'mon."

He turned and began walking down the sidewalk to the corner, followed by Velma, then turned, walked half a block to the alley between the streets, and turned into it. They proceeded down the cracked, broken pavement until they came to the back of Mako's shop.

"Thorough indeed," said Raven grimly, staring at the boards and locks. He turned to Velma. "Keep an eye out."

"For cops?"

"For anybody," he answered. "We're as likely to get held up back here as arrested."

"What do I do if someone starts approaching?" asked Velma.

"Shoot 'em," said Raven. "Well, unless it's a cop."

"Eddie, I don't carry a gun. You know that."

"Okay, if it's a crook, yell 'Rape!' and if it's a cop, do a little dance and cuddle up to him."

She stared at him, frowning. "You're kidding, right?"

"Probably," he said. "Just let me know if someone's coming."

"All right, Eddie."

He reached into his pants pocket, pulled out the small metal instruments he liked to think of as his lock-picking kit, bent over, and went to work. A moment later there was an audible click and he signaled her to enter the shop, then followed her and secured the door behind them.

"So now that we're here, what next?" asked Velma.

"We search for clues."

"What will they look like?"

Raven sighed. "If they don't have C-L-U-E written all over them, we'll just have to use our imaginations." She looked confused and distressed, and he stopped and turned to her. "Look," he said more gently, "someone came here to kill Mako. I assume Rofocale was a regular customer, since he seems to know all about Mako. Now, whoever the shooter was, we have to assume he came here to steal something . . ."

"Why not just to kill Mako?" asked Velma.

"Because if it was just to kill Mako and nothing else, he could have stayed on the sidewalk and shot him through the front window. He couldn't know if Rofocale or I were armed or not, so why take a chance?" Raven shook his head. "No, he *had* to enter the store."

She looked around at the strange Oriental trinkets, the beautifully lettered scrolls, the exquisitely carved animals and people, the elegant swords and daggers, and frowned. "How can we know what's missing?"

"That's why we're detectives," he answered. "We'll figure it out."

"*You're* a detective," she said. "I'm just your secretary."

"You're much more than that, Lisa."

"Velma," she corrected him.

"Velma." He slowly walked behind a counter, to where Mako was standing when he'd been shot, and made a face. "You'd think they'd have wiped the damned bloodstains off the floor. Hell, there's even some on the back of the display case here."

"They probably took a sample, realized it was Mako's blood, or maybe Rofocale's, and decided they didn't need any more," suggested Velma.

"Makes sense," agreed Raven. "I don't suppose any course in police training school specialized in showing them how to mop a floor—or a countertop." He paused. "You're staring at me."

Suddenly she smiled. "If you'd said that mopping up was woman's work, I was going to throw one of these beautifully made daggers at you."

They both chuckled, and he began examining more artifacts. "Have you noticed how almost everything that isn't a scroll or a piece of art is a weapon?" he said. "Most people use a container like this"—he indicated the large vase he was referring to—"for umbrellas. Mako used it for spears."

"And there's a crossbow hanging on the far wall," said Velma. "There are really expensive pieces here, Eddie. It makes sense. I didn't think he could pay for a location like this just by telling fortunes."

"Only if telling fortunes included picking cheap horses who were moving up in class over at Aqueduct," agreed Raven.

"This stuff is all so beautiful and so exotic, I don't know how we'll ever be able to tell what's missing."

"We're not giving up three minutes after we arrive," said Raven. "Someone's dead, and you and Rofocale were in the hospital for weeks."

"Me?" she said, puzzled. "I haven't had a day off in two months."

He grimaced. "My mistake," he said, and then added silently, *Perhaps, but I don't believe it.*

They spent another few minutes going over all the artifacts and opening boxes that were stacked in corners, but kept coming up blank. Finally they'd run through everything and stopped. Velma sat down on the only chair, and Raven leaned against the counter.

"So do we figure this was a dead end?" she asked.

"It may not have been the right approach, but it's not a dead end," answered Raven. "Mako was killed. There's got to be a reason." *And part of that reason might explain why I've been a Munchkin, a Bogart clone, and a sorcerer.*

"You know," remarked Velma, "once you know the stock, as Mako must have, this is really a boring, confining little space. Imagine sitting on this chair eight hours every day."

"Son of a bitch—that's *it*!" exclaimed Raven.

She frowned. "What is? What are you talking about, Eddie?"

"He *didn't* just sit where you are for eight hours a day," said Raven. "If nothing else, he had to visit the bathroom every now and then. And with no hired help, he probably ate right on the premises."

"He could have his food delivered, Eddie. He didn't have to cook it here."

"But he couldn't have his toilet delivered," said Raven. "There's got to be a back room."

They began examining the wall behind the chair and found a door behind the wall hanging. They walked through it and found themselves in a narrow area, perhaps ten feet by five, with a microwave on a shelf and another shelf holding an empty food tray. There was a sink and another door, this time a sliding one, that led to a small toilet.

"Not a lot more comfortable," remarked Velma.

"Not any leads, either," said Raven with a frown. "Yet there *has* to be some reason why he was killed, two of you were shot, and I was left totally alone."

"I wasn't shot," insisted Velma.

"Humor me," said Raven. "The answer's got to be here somewhere . . . or if not the answer, at least a clue." He looked around. "He's got a microwave. He had to store his food somewhere before he cooked it. Where?"

Velma bent down next to the microwave, which sat above a small cabinet. She opened the door to it.

"Here it is, Eddie," she announced. "A tiny freezer. Probably holds half a dozen frozen meals from the grocery store."

"Are there any other cabinets, however small and unimpressive?" asked Raven.

There was one. It held a dozen paper plates, plastic knives, forks, spoons, plastic cups, and a half-empty bottle of ketchup.

"What a way to live!" muttered Raven. "Anything else?"

She looked around. "That's it . . . and I've checked the

drawers out in the shop. Cops left the art, but they took the money."

Raven shrugged. "Cops have to live too, and Mako's not going to need that money where he's at."

"So do we stay or go?"

Raven sighed deeply. "Might as well go. He had his chance to kill us once before. He's not coming back to do it now."

They were just about to leave the tiny room and go back into the store when Raven started to close the door of the washroom and saw something he'd ignored before.

"Just a sec," he said.

"What is it?" asked Velma.

"Medicine cabinet," answered Raven. "It's unlikely that any of this had to do with drugs, but it'll only take me ten seconds to check."

"Go ahead," said Velma.

He entered the little room, opened the cabinet, and froze, staring at what he found inside it.

"What is it, Eddie?" she asked after a moment. "You look like you've seen a ghost."

"Closer than you think," he said, grabbing a piece of paper and carrying it out with him.

"What have you got there?" she asked.

He shrugged helplessly.

"I don't understand," said Velma.

"It means everything I've thought about this was wrong," said Raven.

He held the paper up for her to see.

It was a target-pistol bull's-eye—and superimposed over the bull's-eye was a photo of Eddie Raven.

5

"Whoever it was wanted *you*," said Velma. It was a statement, not a question.

"Absolutely," said Raven, frowning. "But that leaves a major question: Why did he kill Mako, shoot everyone else, and leave me alone?"

"There's only one reasonable answer," said Velma. "You have something, maybe some special knowledge, that they want from you."

"But no one's tried to get it since the shooting."

"Tried *where*, Eddie?" she shot back. "I've been listening to you: Camelot? Oz?"

He grimaced. "Point taken."

"So what's our next move?"

"There's probably nothing more to find out in the shop here," replied Raven. "And I don't feel like going back to my apartment and waiting for them." Once again he found himself fumbling for a cigarette and wishing he had one. "I think it's time for a field trip."

She frowned. "Where to?"

He smiled. "Right here."

"I don't understand," said Velma.

"I've been walking around for a day or two, and I was doing the same thing, visiting the hospital a couple of times a day right after the shooting—and nobody laid a hand on me, no one threatened me or even looked my way. I have a feeling the word has gone out to keep their hands off me. So I plan to confront them and find out who issued the order."

"Confront *who*?" she said, frowning.

"In the comic books and B movies we called them the underworld. These days they're probably the syndicate. I just think of them as the bad guys."

"But they had no reason to shoot you or rough you up, Eddie."

"I know. But someone with some clout doesn't want me killed, and evidently I know something so valuable that they spread around some money or some threats or both to make it so no one shot me by mistake."

"By mistake?"

He smiled. "Do you know how many innocent people get in the way of bullets every day in New York?"

"It's been awhile since anyone accused you of optimism, hasn't it?" she asked, returning his smile.

He patted his pockets. "Only one gun," he said, "and not all that much ammunition. I think I'll go back to the office and pick up a little more protection."

She walked to the door. "Let's go."

"You sure you want to come along?" he asked. "It could be dangerous."

"All the more reason," she said. "Let me have a gun, too."

"I like the way you think, Velma," said Raven, walking out

onto the sidewalk. She joined him, and it took them another fifteen minutes to get back to the office.

Raven walked right to his desk, pulled out two pistols, handed one plus a box of bullets to her, stuck the other in his coat pocket, added some ammunition, and sat down to consider where to go next.

"I'll be right back," said Velma. "Gotta go to the little girls' room."

He nodded an acknowledgment, she left, and he began weighing his options. He noticed that he'd left an empty paper coffee cup on his desk, and reached out to grab it and throw it in the wastebasket, when he noticed his hand. It was far larger than usual, the flesh gnarled, covered by coarse, matted hair, and with gleaming inch-long nails.

"Shit!" he muttered, walking over to stare at his image in the glass on the office door. "I thought I was all through being other people."

He looked at the face staring out at him. It was that of a dead man, the eyes hollow and staring, big ugly stitches on the neck, the hair sparse and long.

He turned to see if Velma had come back yet, and was relieved to find that she hadn't. He couldn't ask or expect her to come along with Frankenstein's monster or whatever the hell he'd become, and even if she was willing to, he didn't want her anywhere near him when the shooting started, as it almost certainly would when anyone saw what he had become.

He grabbed his battered fedora, pulled it down almost to his eyes, lowered his head, walked out the door, and quickly made his way to the subway station on the corner. He went down the stairs, grateful for the lack of human traffic, then walked to the far end of the platform, made sure no one was watching him, and jumped down onto the area between the tracks.

He walked another hundred yards, stopped, crossed over the tracks to his right, and came to a door. He had no idea how he had known it was there, but he had, and now he entered it.

When he was two feet inside the entrance, he stopped, frowning.

Since there's likely to be some shooting, I'd better see if bullets can do me any harm. I think I'm dead, but let me at least see if I've got a pulse.

He felt for one and couldn't find it.

Well, that's a good thing, I suppose.

He began walking down a dark corridor, came to a door in about fifty feet, felt around for a knob or a handle, found it, opened the door, and stepped into a well-lit room filled with chairs, couches, a wet bar, a sink, clouds of cigarette and cigar smoke, and seven men, some of whom he recognized from newscasts or their posters.

"Hi, guys," he said in a voice that was about two octaves lower than his own.

Suddenly all seven men were on their feet. Two of them, the two closest, who had the best view of him, were shaking like leaves, but all seven had guns in their hands, and all were pointing at him.

"I mean you no harm," said Raven. "I just want to talk."

"Who and what are you?" demanded one of them.

"My name's Frankie," he answered. "I'm a friend of Eddie Raven. He was expecting this kind of reception, so he asked me to come in his place."

"I repeat: What *are* you?"

"I'm just a guy who needs to talk to you."

"You're not a guy at all," said another. "What graveyard did you escape from?"

"It's a long story," said Raven. "Someone's after my friend Eddie Raven. We have reason to believe that he's located in Manhattan. We just want to find out who and where he is. No harm will come to you if you help me out on this."

"There's plenty of harm in this room," said a third man, "and it ain't coming to *us*, baby!"

And so saying, he put three bullets into Raven's chest.

Suddenly Raven smiled—a smile of relief, though none of them could tell that. "It tickles," he said.

The shooter examined his pistol, then looked up, frowning. "It's working."

"Now, you can all empty your guns into me, if it'll make you happy, but then we're going to talk, and if I have to wait too long I suspect I'll be in a very bad mood."

The seven men exchanged looks.

"Have a drink, Frankie," said one of them. "We're happy to talk."

Raven walked to the bar, poured himself a drink, took a swallow, and felt half of it roll out through a couple of bullet holes in his neck. The other half went down, but somehow didn't taste quite right.

"Now," he said, "our information is that there's a hit out on Eddie Raven. We don't know the connection, but we think it may have something to do with the guy who shot up that fortune-teller's shop over on Fifth Avenue a few weeks ago."

"Got a question," said one of the man.

"Shoot," said Raven. Five men leveled their weapons at him. "Make that *ask*."

"How did you know we were down here?"

Raven smiled. "I'm a detective, remember?"

"You're a critter out of my worst DTs, but you're no detective!"

Damn! thought Raven. *Remember who and what you are, Eddie.*

"Okay," he said aloud. "Eddie kind of deputized me. *He's* the detective, and it's his business to know where to find you."

"Got another question," said the man. "The bullets didn't hurt you, but did you know they left little holes in you where they hit?"

"So what?" asked Raven, trying to see where the conversation was going.

"So," said the man, pointing his gun at Raven's head, "maybe we can't kill you, but you'll have a damned difficult time finding us after we shoot your eyes out."

And suddenly seven guns were pointed at his eyes.

"Oh, I wouldn't do that if I were you," said a feminine voice from the doorway.

Raven and the seven men turned toward the doorway, where they saw a medusa, a female creature with hair made of living snakes, each baring its fangs at them. In her hands she carried a spear gun, but instead of a spear it housed a snake that hissed incessantly and exhaled flames.

"Lisa?" whispered Raven.

She smiled a frightening smile and shook her head. "Euryale."

"It's a goddamned medusa!" said the man who was closest to her.

"Medusa's my puny kid sister," she replied with a smile. "Now I suggest you put your pistols down before I take them away from you and feed them to my snakes."

One of the men fired a quick shot at her. It bounced off her cheek, rebounded into the closest man, and knocked him down.

"You heard what the lady said," said the shooter. "Holster your guns."

Six men put their guns away, while the seventh got painfully to his feet, checked to make sure all his bodily parts were still attached and functioning, and handed his gun to Euryale.

"All right," she said, "I believe you gentlemen were preparing to answer my friend's questions?"

"I don't know why you care," said one of the men. "Bullets bounce off one of you, and go to sleep inside the other."

"We're doing this for my friend Eddie Raven," said Raven. "And now, if you're all through doubting our abilities, I'd like some answers."

"Hell, the last few minutes have been so crazy I don't even remember the question."

"Who wants Eddie Raven dead, and why? And what does it have to do with Mako or his fortune-telling shop?"

"I don't know," said the closest man. "Just that word came down a couple of months ago to keep our hands off Raven."

"This was before the shooting?"

"Definitely."

"And who passed the word?"

The man shrugged. "Beats me. We all got it."

"By 'all' do you mean you seven?"

The man shook his head. "I mean every crook in our organization, which extends into Brooklyn and Queens and the whole city. And that was the gist of it: Leave Raven alone."

Raven frowned and turned to Euryale. "Is he telling the truth?"

She gave the man a frightening smile. "He'd better be."

Raven looked at the men. "Anything else?"

"Yeah," said the man who'd been sprawling on the floor a couple of minutes earlier. "There's one thing that might be of some interest or use or import or something."

"Okay," said Raven. "What is it?"

"The organization put out a hit on Raven about three or four months ago. In fact, he was number one on our enemies list. The word went out to everyone, however many thousands of us there are: Kill Eddie Raven. Then, a couple of weeks later, maybe a month at most, word came down to leave him totally alone." He paused. "Make any sense to you, Frankie?"

"Sounds like we're going to have to go a little higher in the ranks for our answers," said Raven. "Who's the top man?"

"We just know him as Mister Big," was the reply.

"And where do I find him?"

"He'll kill me—all of us—if I tell you."

"And I'll give you a passionate hug and kiss if you don't," said Euryale. "Which do you think is more agonizing?"

The man rattled off an address.

"This had better not be a phony," said Raven. "We know where to find you."

"You don't think we'll still be here tomorrow, or even an hour from now?" said another of the men.

"No, I don't," answered Raven. "But then, you don't really think you can stay hidden from us, do you?"

The man looked at Raven and Lisa in their current incarnations and simply shook his head.

"Then, if you'll excuse us for intruding on your party, we'll be on our way," said Raven, walking to the door.

"Bon voyage," said the smallest man. "Have a safe trip, Frankie."

Raven walked out the door and back into the subway tunnel. He waited for his companion to follow him, then turned to her.

"Shut the door, Lisa," he said.

She frowned. "My name is Euryale," she said.

6

"It's happened again," muttered Raven.

"What has?" she asked.

He almost did a double-take. "Look at us!"

She nodded. "I should have fed my hair. It's too active."

"Goddamnit!"

"Try to control yourself, Frankie."

"I'm Eddie," he growled. "Eddie Raven. You *know* that."

She shrugged. "If that's what you want to be called, fine."

"What the hell's going on?" he demanded. "We were just in my office a couple of hours ago, and then at Mako's shop."

She stared at him. "I've never been in an office, and I don't know who Mako is."

"Then what are you doing down here in the subway?"

"Following you, of course."

"Why?" he insisted.

"We're a team—Frankie and Euryale."

"I've read the book. The monster was never called Frankenstein, not once."

"What book?" she shot back. "You've always been Frankie to me, just as I've always been Euryale to you. At least until you called me that other name a moment ago."

"Lisa?"

She nodded, causing her hair to hiss and writhe. "That's the one."

He stared at her for a long moment. "Okay, Euryale, what did we do yesterday?"

A smile of reminiscence crossed her face. "How could you forget, Frankie? We terrorized a whole kindergarten class of goblins."

He frowned. "We did?"

She chuckled. "I'll bet they obey their parents *now*."

"Okay," he said. "And the day before that?"

"That was the highlight of our week, Frankie. Don't you remember how we saved the manticore before the mob could tear it to pieces?"

A sense of relief swept over Raven. "So we're basically Good Guys. We just *look* like monsters."

"Speak for yourself," said Euryale. "*I* think I look pretty good." She struck a pose that would have elicited wolf whistles if she was Lisa, but was mildly terrifying when assumed by a heavily weaponized medusa.

"I misspoke," he said, and hoped his nose didn't instantly grow six or seven inches.

"We're a team, and a damned good one," she replied.

"Then maybe we'd better get back to work," he said.

"What exactly are we doing?" she asked. "It's so pleasant down here," she added, waving a hand at the dark, damp, bleak surroundings, "that I almost forgot we're working."

"We're trying to discover who put out the kill order on Eddie Raven," he answered. "And since there *was* a kill order, why the shooter killed Mako and seriously wounded two others, and never even took a shot at Raven."

"He sounds like a very confused man," offered Euryale.

"It's more than him," said Raven. "Or bigger than him. Or something along those lines."

"I don't follow you, Frankie."

"I . . . make that *Raven* . . . never got near him. I found the kill order weeks later, hidden inside Mako's kitchen. Which means . . ."

". . . that the kill order went out to more than one party," she concluded. Then she frowned. "But if that was the case, why didn't Mako kill Eddie Raven the moment he entered Mako's shop?"

"Beats the hell out of me. These are all things we have to find out."

"Sounds like fun," she said. "By the way, who's paying us for all this?"

He paused for a moment, then came up with the only answer he thought she would accept. "Eddie Raven."

She nodded her head. "Makes sense. So what's our next step?"

"I haven't eaten all day," said Raven. "How about you?"

The snakes all began hissing and writhing wildly.

"Frankie, I've asked you never to mention f-o-o-d in front of my hair."

"Sorry," he said.

"Anyway, I could go for some."

"Good," he said. Suddenly he found himself staring at her hair. "Any suggestions?"

"The usual place," answered Euryale.

"Lead the way," he said.

She turned and began walking until she came to a well-hidden, very narrow stairway about two hundred yards away. She then ascended halfway to street level, followed a corridor for another fifty feet, and came to a small room. Three sides were brick and one side glass, with a door in the middle of the glass, and she entered.

Raven followed her, and tried not to pay attention to the screams and curses coming from the kitchen, since it was clear to him that they were not emanating from human throats.

She sat down in a booth that looked to him like it was covered with skin. Raven wanted to think it was animal skin, but then he saw the remnants of some tattoos on it.

"We come here often, do we?" he asked.

She nodded, which upset a few of the snakes. "It's easier than finding one restaurant for me and one for my hair."

A hunchbacked waiter limped over to their table, carrying a sword.

"Welcome back, Euryale."

"Hi, Igor," she said. "We're good and hungry."

"Just you and Frankie?" he asked.

"*All* of us."

"Okay," he said, nodding his mildly misshapen head. "What'll it be?"

"The usual," she said.

"Fine," he said. He tucked the sword into a sheath. "Then you won't be needing this."

He walked off to the kitchen, and Raven turned to Euryale.

"You kill your own food here?" he asked disbelievingly.

She shrugged. "Sometimes my hair likes to play with its dinner. Problem is, it can get very messy."

"I can imagine," he said, and then corrected himself. "No, I *can't* imagine, and I'm much happier that way."

"You're acting oddly today, Frankie," said Euryale. "Why, the last time we were here, you were betting other customers on which of my follicles would deliver the death blow."

Suddenly they heard an inhuman scream coming from the kitchen.

"What the hell was that?" muttered Raven.

"It could be anything from the cook burning himself to the cook burning whatever they're eating at the next table."

Raven frowned. "Has this place got a name?"

"Originally it was Eat at Joe's," she said.

"Originally?"

"Then the new owners took it over."

"And what is it now?" asked Raven.

"Almost the same."

"Eat at Joe's?"

"Eat Joe," she answered. "Though I don't suppose there's been anything left of Joe for some months now."

Raven was about to voice his disgust when it occurred to him that a sandwich of Joe on rye bread sounded pretty tasty at the moment. He decided that if he watched Euryale's snakes rip apart and gobble their dinner, whatever it was, it might do serious damage to his appetite, so he simply signaled Igor over and ordered a beer.

"With or without?" asked Igor.

"With or without what?" asked Raven cautiously.

"Blood of an Innocent," was the answer.

"An Innocent *what*?" asked Raven.

Igor shrugged. "I'll have to see what we've got back there that's still alive and kicking." A sudden scream echoed through the building. "Or yelling."

"How about just a glass of water?"

"Same question, pal," said Igor. "With or without?"

"*Just* water," said Raven firmly.

Igor shook his head in wonderment. "Boy, we sure get our share of weirdos in here," he said as he walked back to the kitchen.

"You look upset, Frankie," said Euryale, reaching over and laying her hand on his. "We'll get to the bottom of this, never fear."

"Of dinner?" he said, frowning. "I hope not."

"The case," she said. "The one or more guys who may or may not want to kill Eddie Raven—and why one of them shot his friends instead."

"Only one of them was his friend. He'd never seen the other two before."

"Very strange," she said, frowning beneath the snakes that served as bangs. "Everything about this case is weird."

"An understatement," agreed Raven.

"For instance, where *is* this Eddie Raven? And why haven't we spoken to the two people who survived being shot?"

He wanted to say, *I'm speaking to one of them right now,* but of course he didn't.

Dinner, such as it was, arrived a moment later, preceded by unearthly screaming and howling, and Raven tried to look away while her hair played with its dinner—but everywhere he looked he encountered a more frightening sight. Finally he just leaned back, closed his eyes, waited for the last scream to end very suddenly, and sighed deeply.

"I've been to a lot of places recently," he remarked. "In fact, I've been a lot of people. But this is definitely the strangest."

"Isn't it thrilling?" Euryale said enthusiastically.

"That's one word for it," replied Raven. "Not the one that pops to mind ahead of all others, but what the hell."

Two of the larger hair follicles got into a spat over the last piece of dinner, the larger one won, and Euryale turned to Raven.

"Okay, Frankie," she said. "We're sated now."

"We?" said Raven, frowning.

"My hair and me," she answered. "Let's go catch the bad guys."

"Given our surroundings, maybe we'd better define them first."

"I have an even better idea," offered Igor, approaching them. "Pay for your dinner first."

Raven reached into a pocket, fumbled around for a few seconds, and withdrew a bill.

"We don't want your money, pal," said Igor.

Raven frowned. "What *do* you want?"

Igor looked down at the hand. "Oh, a thumb and a forefinger ought to do it."

"They came in here with me and they're leaving with me," growled Raven. "Now you can take the five I'm offering you, or you can take my spare comb, but that's your only choice."

"Why do you have a spare comb?" asked Igor curiously. "You've barely got enough hair to merit *one* comb."

*It would take too long to explain that it's Eddie Raven's comb
and it made the transition with me.*

"I live in hope," replied Raven.

"You've come to the wrong place," said Igor. "Around here,
people die in hope." He paused thoughtfully for a moment.
"Or without it," he added.

"One of them's going to die without his fingers if he grabs
for anything but the bill," said Raven.

Igor looked at the five-dollar bill, then at the unforgiving
expression on Raven's monstrous face, and finally sighed,
grabbed the bill, and retreated to the kitchen.

"I hope they'll let you come back here," Raven said to Euryale.

"Why wouldn't they?" she asked.

He jerked his head in Igor's direction. "Him."

She smiled. "Not to worry. He'll probably be on the menu
next month." She paused, then added thoughtfully, "Maybe
sooner."

"Ready to go?" he asked her.

"Yes," she said. "I need some external diversions."

He stared at her with a puzzled expression.

"My hair," she explained. "It's starting to snore."

"Ah!" he replied. "Okay, let's go."

They walked out of the restaurant, back into the tunnel,
and then the subway.

"Damn!" he muttered. "I forgot."

"Your wallet?" she asked.

He shook his head. "Our appearance. We can't go back up
on the sidewalk in the middle of Manhattan looking like this."

She stared at him, frowning. "Your shirt's not that dirty,
Frankie."

"It's not a matter of clean or dirty," replied Raven. "It's a matter of blending in or scaring the hell out of people."

Not to worry, Eddie. You've still got a mission to accomplish.

Raven froze, concentrating, but there wasn't anything more. Finally he looked over at Euryale.

"Was that you?" he asked.

"I don't think so," she said, frowning. "What do you think I did?"

"Kind of whispered into my mind."

"I was thinking how much better you looked than Boris Karloff," she replied. "Is *that* what you heard?"

He shook his head. "No, definitely not."

She shrugged. "Then it wasn't me."

Rofocale? thought Raven. *Are you conscious again?*

Just barely, came Rofocale's reply.

What did you mean? I know I have a mission to accomplish.

I meant that you can't accomplish it in the subway system, fifty feet under the ground.

I can't show myself like this, answered Raven.

I know.

Well then?

You won't have to, Eddie. Just climb up to ground level and step outside, and you'll be Eddie Raven again.

And—he tried to decide what name to call her, then realized they were still on a case—*Velma?*

She'll be as she was.

Okay, said Raven. *Is there anything else I should know?*

Just one thing, answered Rofocale.

And what is that?

Time's running short.

They reached street level, walked to a door, and opened it. "What the hell is going on here?" muttered Raven. "Where's the city?"

He looked down the dirt street, past a few horse-drawn carriages, then turned to his companion.

"You're Lisa again!" he exclaimed.

"I'm Elizabeth," she replied.

He looked at his hands, which seemed normal, then felt his face.

"And I'm not a monster anymore!"

"You never really were," she said.

"Still, it's good to be Eddie Raven again!"

She shook her head. "You're not, I'm afraid."

He frowned, looked around for a mirror or something else that would reflect his image, saw a storefront window behind him, walked over to it, and stared.

"That's me," he said. "I just don't wear these kinds of clothes."

"Those are precisely what you wear," she said.

"And you don't wear high-necked floor-length dresses," he continued.

"I most certainly do."

"What the hell is going on?" demanded Raven. "Where the hell *are* we?"

"We are in Meryton, in Hertfordshire," she replied, "and please watch your language. You're starting to attract stares, Mister—"

"It's Eddie," he interrupted her. "We've been through too much together to be so formal."

"Actually, it's Fitzwilliam," she said. "But it's far more proper for me to call you Mr. Darcy."

Where have I seen or heard those names before? thought Raven. *Fitzwilliam Darcy and Elizabeth . . . Elizabeth who?* He shut his eyes for a moment and concentrated. *Son of a bitch! It's Elizabeth Bennet, and we're living in Jane Austen's* Pride and Prejudice*!*

"Suddenly you look happy," she said.

"That's because I've figured out who and where we are," he replied.

"I didn't know it was a mystery."

"There are bigger mysteries than that," he said. "At least I don't have to solve them while I'm Frankenstein's monster or its near cousin."

"I have no idea what you're talking about, Mr. Darcy."

"Not to worry, Elizabeth," he replied. "As long as *I* know." He noticed her frowning. "What's the problem?"

"You should address me as Miss Bennet."

"My mistake," he said. "How about if I just call you Lisa?"

She frowned and made no reply.

"No, huh?" he said.

She turned and looked at the public building behind them,

and half smiled. "I think you left all your manners on the other side of that door, Mr. Darcy."

"So I take it you don't want to call me Eddie either?"

She simply stared at him in silence.

"I thought not," he said. He looked up and down the street, frowning.

"What seems to be the problem, Mr. Darcy?"

"Same as usual," he replied. "Trying to figure out how to get home from here."

"What *is* the matter with you, Mr. Darcy?"

"You got a pen and a thick notepad?" he responded.

"Does this pass for humor among London's fashionable set?" she asked.

"God, I hope not," said Raven. He sighed, looked around at what appeared to be the very small town, and turned back to her. "So may I walk you home, Miss Bennet?"

"All four miles?" she replied.

"Why don't I hire a carriage?"

"Didn't you bring your own carriage, or at least your horse?" she asked. "Your estate is some two hundred miles farther out in the country than mine."

Think of a good answer, Eddie, he told himself. *She's already got her doubts about you. Convince her that you don't know where either of you live or how to get there and she'll walk away and leave you alone in a land that seems as unfamiliar as Oz or Camelot.*

"My horse seemed a bit sore," said Raven at last. "I don't want to take a chance on his becoming lame. I thought I'd give him a few hours to relax and see if he's any better later in the day."

She nodded her approval. "Very sensible," she said. "I just

hope we can get him to home, or at least some shelter, before nightfall brings the ravening hordes again."

The ravening hordes? Raven bit his lip just as he was about to ask what she was referring to. *Play it by ear, Eddie,* he told himself. *The one thing you can't do is scare her off before you learn the ground rules to this place.*

"I'll make sure he's well protected," said Raven aloud. "What about you and your family?"

"We're probably safe," she replied, then paused, considered what she had said, and repeated the word. "Probably."

"Oh?"

"George Wickham, whatever he actually is, seems taken with my sister Jane. I don't imagine he would kill the rest of the family to impress her."

"That seems a reasonable assumption," agreed Raven.

"I would hope so, but how can one know, given what he becomes at night?"

One more line like that and I'm going to have to start asking questions, thought Raven.

"Well, I hope everyone's defenses are up," he said.

"How does one defend against dozens of monsters on horseback?" she replied. "You just hope they're after someone else, or that you're so difficult to find that they go after easier targets, or—"

"I get the idea," he said, reaching out and holding her hand. He half expected her to shudder, or at least tell him to let go, but instead she looked at him and smiled.

"We'll survive," she said. "We were fine before Wickham and his horde discovered Meryton, and we'll be fine after he moves on to greener pastures."

"Or until someone stops him," said Raven.

She looked at him and offered him a sad little smile. "If someone could, they'd already have done it."

He spotted a small tea shop across the street, put a hand in his pocket to make sure he had money, and resisted the urge to see what two-century-old currency looked like.

"Come on," he said, offering her his arm. "I'll buy you a cup of . . . tea." *Damn! Gotta watch it! Almost said "coffee."*

She took his arm and they walked to the tea shop, then sat at a small table by a window.

"If you'd like something else, or something *more*, you've but to ask," he said, hoping he sounded like a civilized country gentleman.

"Tea will be quite sufficient," she replied.

He signaled to a servant, they ordered, and then he closed his eyes for a moment and concentrated.

If you're there, Rofocale, I could use some help, or at least some advice. What the hell am I doing in a Jane Austen novel?

If she is right about Wickham and his creatures, it's not a Jane Austen novel, came the answer.

You're awake! thought Raven excitedly.

Briefly.

What the hell am I doing here, and how do I get back to my *New York and the* real *Lisa?*

There are some things I can't tell you, Eddie, replied Rofocale, *and some I won't tell you. You have skills and abilities of which you remain unaware, which you haven't yet drawn upon—and you have a unique destiny.*

What are you talking about? I've been a Munchkin and a wizard and a monster. How the hell much more unique can my destiny be? Can't you at least tell me why this is happening to me?

Telling you would not help, Eddie.

Why don't you tell me and let me decide?

All will become clear to you before too much longer. In the meantime, to borrow one of your own expressions, you must play it by ear.

You've got to tell me a little more than that, demanded Raven.

But there was no answer, and somehow he knew that, unlike the last few times they'd been in contact, Rofocale hadn't passed out or gone back into a coma, but had simply chosen to break the connection.

"Are you quite all right, Mr. Darcy?"

He blinked and looked across the table, where Lisa/Elizabeth was staring at him with some concern.

He grimaced. "Daydreaming," he said. "A bad habit. I apologize."

"I'm just glad to know you're all right," she replied. "You had me quite concerned for a moment."

"I'll try not to do it again," answered Raven.

The servant arrived with the tea.

"Thanks," said Raven. "How much will it be?"

"The usual," was his answer.

He reached into his pocket, pulled out a bill, and handed it to the waiter.

"Thank you, sir!" said the waiter with a huge smile.

Oh, shit, thought Raven. *Next time I'd better look—but what the hell do I know about what any denomination is worth in this era?*

"One of the things I admire about you, Mr. Darcy," said Elizabeth, "is that you are generous with both your time and your money. So many men in your position hoard what they have, when it is capable of bringing so much joy to so many without doing any noticeable harm to your own standing."

He stared at her for a long moment. *You know,* he found himself thinking, *this is a beautiful little town, a much simpler era, I'm filthy rich, and whatever she calls herself, she's my Lisa. I could stay here forever.*

Then he remembered that forever could be ending in another eight or ten hours if he didn't make preparations to survive Wickham and whatever constituted his hordes.

Ah, well, we'll kill all the bad guys, especially the one who shot you back in New York, and then live happily ever after.

"I wish it was as easy as you make it sound."

He stared across the table. "Did you say something, Lisa?"

"No," she replied. "And it's *Elizabeth.*"

Rofocale, I know you don't want to talk, but just tell me: Was that her?

Possibly, came the answer.

8

"It's getting late," noted Raven. "We'd better be going. I think we can defend ourselves better at Pemberley."

She shook her head. "That would feel like I was deserting my parents and my sisters," she said.

Suddenly they heard wild, inhuman screams from no more than a mile away.

"That settles *that*," said Raven. "We'd better find someplace to hide right here and hope they're not looking for townspeople."

"They're looking for *anyone*," she replied, frowning. "You know that."

"True," he said quickly. "I was just hoping aloud."

"I understand Mr. Bingley had some business in town today," said Elizabeth. "Perhaps we can join up with him."

The screams came closer, and Raven shook his head. "There's no time to go hunting for anyone," he replied. "Let's get out of sight."

He stood up, held out his hand, and led her to the kitchen, where the cook and the waiter stood trembling.

There were more screams, and then they heard a body crash against the front door. Raven cracked open the kitchen door and took a look. A blood-spattered young man lay in the doorway, breathing his last.

Suddenly they heard a rifle shot.

This is crazy, thought Raven. *There's been more violence in the past two minutes than Jane Austen put in her entire literary output.*

"I know you're in there, Darcy!" cried a voice.

"Wickham!" whispered Elizabeth.

"What the hell does he want with me?" wondered Raven aloud.

"You exposed his sins and weaknesses to my family when he was courting my sister," said Elizabeth. "He's never forgiven you for it."

"You come out, Darcy, or my creatures will burn the place—and everyone who's in it—down."

"Shit!" muttered Raven. He turned to the cook and waiter. "Anyone got a gun?"

They both shook their heads, too frightened to speak.

"Okay," he said. "How about a butcher knife?"

The chef reached for one, grabbed it, and handed it to Raven.

"You're not really going out there, are you?" asked Elizabeth.

"No choice," answered Raven. "If I don't, he kills all four of us."

"Don't go!" she said.

"I have to."

"Please, Eddie."

Suddenly he froze. "You called me *Eddie!*"

"Please stay!"

"I'll be back," he promised, and walked out of the kitchen. He made his way through the restaurant, avoiding the dead body, and stepped out into the street.

Facing him was a lean, well-groomed, well-dressed man on a chestnut horse . . . and forty creatures, all on their bare misshapen feet, all ashen-white, all with cold, dead eyes and discolored pointed teeth, who may once have been men, though certainly not in years, probably decades.

"I knew I'd find you here, Darcy," said Wickham, clearly enjoying his moment of triumph.

"Even you aren't stupid enough not to find me in a village this size," replied Raven. "Now what do you and your pets want?"

"Did you hear that?" yelled Wickham to his horde. "He called you my pets!"

"You give orders and they obey you," replied Raven. "Isn't that what pets do?"

The creatures began looking uneasy.

"Of course," continued Raven, "you can beat them and belittle them and abuse them, and they'll still obey you. I mean," he added, "it's not as if they can, or even could, think for themselves."

The creatures began muttering uneasily.

"Listen to him!" yelled Wickham with a harsh laugh. "He thinks he can argue you into disobeying my commands!"

"Of course not," said Raven. "Why should they disobey you? I mean, hell, when all is said and done, you hold the power of life and death over them." He paused, and the hint of a smile played on his lips. "Don't you?"

Now the muttering began in earnest.

"Be careful not to get him mad," continued Raven. "He's just the type who would be happy to poison your food if you enrage him—and of course he has access to every last piece of it. I mean, he *does* feed you and pay you and give you all kinds of rewards for the service you render him." And in case there were any French creatures in the group, he concluded with a smile and a *"N'est ce pas?"*

"Shut your mouth, Darcy!" screamed Wickham. "Or I'll cut your tongue out of your mouth *before* I kill you."

Raven smiled and addressed the horde. "Is that why none of you talk back to him? Is he a tongue collector? Think he'll collect your eyeballs next?"

He could tell they were considering what he said. He fell silent for a moment, not because of Wickham's threats, but because he doubted the creatures could assimilate any more.

"You've been begging for this, Darcy!" growled Wickham, sword in one hand and war club in the other.

"Begging for it?" said Raven, frowning. "I'm been in this world half a day."

"And after I cut you into ribbons and feed you to my troops, I'm going to do the same thing with your lady."

Raven turned to see Elizabeth's reaction, but she just stared at Wickham with an expression, not of loathing, but rather extreme distaste, as if he was too low on the evolutionary scale to elicit any stronger reaction.

"And when I'm through with her," continued Wickham, "I'll feed her to my noble army!"

"There's not all that much of her to begin with," said Raven to the creatures, "let alone enough to share in forty or fifty equal portions. If I was looking for a bigger, better meal, I'd look over there." He jerked his thumb in Wickham's direction.

There were some mumbled assents, and Wickham began twitching nervously.

"Are you going to listen to him, or to the noble leader who has led you time and again into glorious and victorious battle?" he screamed.

"He's got a point," agreed Raven. "And surely he's shared the spoils of battle with you. I mean, you all have fine new weapons and uniforms, don't you? And you walk barefoot on unpaved and rocky roads while he leads you on horseback." He paused. "I mean, he *does* lead you into battle, doesn't he? He doesn't hold back while you kill the most dangerous of the enemy's army."

Now they began muttering in earnest again.

Raven grinned and turned to Wickham. "Seriously, wouldn't you rather go home and think about it for a while?"

"I've been thinking about killing you for more than a while," muttered Wickham.

"Why?" said Raven. "What the hell have I ever done to you?"

"You mean in *this* life?" shot back Wickham. "You tried to break up my pending marriage to one of the Bennet girls—the good-looking one."

"What kind of answer is that?" demanded Raven. "In this life? How many lives have you got?"

"Enough," muttered Wickham. "And I loathe you in all of them."

Raven frowned and stared at the man. There was something vaguely familiar about him, something he couldn't quite put his finger on. But it wasn't in this guise, in this milieu.

Rofocale, are you there?

No answer.

Rofocale, this is important. Look through my eyes and tell me where I've seen this guy before.

There was no answer.

Thanks, was Raven's bitter thought. *It would have been nice to know who the hell he is before he butchers me.*

Raven tightened his grip on the knife and took a step forward.

"Okay," he said grimly, trying not to compare the knife with Wickham's weapons. "Let's get this over with."

Suddenly he heard a female voice scream.

"Oh my God, Eddie! He's the shooter from Mako's!"

Wickham muttered a curse, one never before heard in that century, and vanished. One instant he was there, swinging his sword; the next instant he was gone.

Raven turned to the source of the scream.

"Lisa?" he half said, half whispered.

She nodded and held out her hand. "It's time to go, Eddie."

"Where?" he asked, taking her hand and giving it a gentle squeeze.

"Anywhere but here," she said just before they vanished.

9

Raven experienced a moment of utter cold and darkness. Then he opened his eyes and found himself back in his apartment. He looked around for Lisa, but she wasn't there.

He phoned the hospital, learned that she'd been released, and dialed her number, only to be told by an electronic voice that no such number existed.

How could I forget it?

He hunted up the phone book and looked for her name. It wasn't there. Then he tried Information, which was unable to help him.

"What the hell is going on?" he muttered.

In quick order he tried to find a listing for the Eddie Raven Detective Agency and the underworld bar where he and Lisa had gone as Frankie and Euryale. No luck.

He walked into the bathroom and stared at the mirror.

"Same face I've seen since I was kid," he said. He continued staring intently. "I don't *look* crazy." He sighed deeply. "But what sane man spends time as a man-made monster and an elegant Jane Austen character, to say nothing of the ones that came before? Damn it, Lisa, right at the end you knew the answer. Where are you now?"

Well, if you can't give me the answers I need, there's one person who can—always assuming he's still alive and hopefully awake. Raven frowned and concentrated. *Rofocale, are you there?*

No response.

Damn it, Rofocale—wake up, or come back to life, or whatever. I need some answers.

He sensed that Rofocale was there—wherever *there* was—but he couldn't elicit a response.

He tried the phone book, and Information, and got the same response he'd received when asking for Lisa.

So am I stuck here until I'm transformed into something else that makes no sense—or until someone or something tries to kill me?

He sat perfectly still, eyes shut, fists opening and closing as his hands rested on the desk.

Maybe, just maybe, there's another way to go about this. This guy's got to be on record somewhere, if only as a physical freak.

He had a friend who worked for the police check to see if a Lucifuge Rofocale was wanted anywhere. The answer was no. He called the Secret Service and asked if they wanted a lead on the whereabouts of Lucifuge Rofocale. They'd never heard of him. Finally, he activated his laptop, brought up Google, and typed in the name Lucifuge Rofocale.

And even after all he'd been through, the response still startled him: *Lucifuge Rofocale is the head of Hell's Government—named by the Dark Prince himself in recognition of The Rofocale's competence.*

Raven half frowned and half grimaced. "You're kidding!" he

muttered. Then he thought back over the last couple of weeks—his incarnations in Casablanca and Oz and Camelot and Africa, as a detective and a monster and a British gentleman—and he realized that the computer wasn't kidding at all.

"But why *me*?" he muttered. "I haven't lived a perfect life, but I've never hurt anyone, at least not knowingly, I haven't committed any felonies, I've just been a goddamned clothes merchant in the Garment District since I quit college. There's got to have been a mistake!"

I don't make mistakes, Eddie, Rofocale's thought came to him, weak but identifiable. *Not of that magnitude.*

"What the hell do you want of me?" demanded Raven, half shouting into the empty room.

You'll know soon enough.

Soon enough isn't *soon enough,* thought Raven. *Tell me now, damn it!*

He felt a mental chuckle at the other end of the connection.

Didn't anyone ever tell you not to curse at a demon, Eddie?

Just tell me what the hell is going on, and what I have to do with it, or what it has to do with me!

Patience, Eddie.

Raven could tell the connection was broken.

He spent a couple of minutes considering his options. When he eliminated those that were clearly not viable, he was left with only one: walk over to Rofocale's room and find some way to get answers out of him, by clever questions if possible, or by physical force if necessary.

He got to his feet, walked to his closet, and pulled out his jacket.

"Damn it!" he muttered. "I always thought I was one of the good guys. Am I a demon, too?"

"Never forget," said a familiar voice, "that a demon is merely a fallen angel."

He turned and found himself facing Lisa, who was dressed in an elegant, flowing white gown.

"Don't be afraid, Eddie," she said. "I am here to assuage your fears, not to exacerbate them."

"I didn't see you come in," he said.

She smiled. "I didn't use the door."

"You just somehow appeared?"

"If you say so."

"So *am* I a demon?"

She smiled enigmatically. "It's one of the infinite number of things you might be, given the choices you make."

"You're making about as much sense as Rofocale," said Raven.

"Maybe you're just misunderstanding me as much," she replied.

"Look," he said, "if I'm *not* a demon, or not yet one, why is everyone trying to kill me?"

"*Think*, Eddie," she exhorted him. "If you saw Hitler as a small boy, if you *knew* it was Hitler, would you wait for him to grow to adulthood before killing him, or would you save six million lives and kill him now?"

"I'm *that* evil?" he asked with a sick feeling at the pit of his stomach.

"Calm down, Eddie," she said, reaching out and gently holding his hand. "It was merely an example."

"If Lucifuge Rofocale is trying to protect me," he said, "then maybe I *should* be killed."

She sighed. "Not everything is as it appears to you," she said. "You must trust me on this."

He stared at her, but said nothing.

"I will help you sort out truth from lies, and greater truths from lesser truths, as you continue your quest."

"What quest?" he demanded. "And while we're at it, who *are* you? Clearly you're not Lisa."

"I am *also* Lisa," she replied, still holding his hand. "And I have been drawn to you as you have been drawn to me from the first moment that we met almost two years ago."

"You're ducking my question," said Raven. "Who *are* you?"

"You're a bright man, Eddie," she replied. "I should have thought the answer would be obvious."

And as the words left her mouth she became an exotic Asian girl dressed in a blue velvet gown.

"I am the Mistress of Illusions," she continued. "Great powers are aligned against you, Eddie Raven. I will help you sort through the maze of intrigue and misdirection they have set in your path."

Raven frowned. "But why?" he asked at last. "What am I expected to do if I survive?"

"The same thing you would do if you were really the detective you were pretending to be," she answered. "Put the villains where they can do no more harm. Or if you were Mordred, magic them away. If you were Alan Quatermain, line them up in your sights and pull the trigger. Or . . ."

"I get the picture," he said. "So am I a hero or a villain?"

"Everyone's a villain to someone," said Lisa.

"You're driving me crazy!" he snapped in frustration. "Can't I get a straight answer?"

"Not from the Mistress of Illusions," she replied with a gentle smile that seemed tinged with sadness or regret. As she spoke, she changed form again, this time into a gorgeous peasant girl from the Russian steppes. "You must learn to interpret, Eddie, and to intuit, if you—and all the worlds that coexist with yours—are to survive."

"Mine, not ours?"

"I don't follow you."

"This world," said Raven. "Isn't it yours too?"

"It is while I'm on it, interacting with you. And when we are on another world, or in another reality, then that will be mine for as long as we reside upon it."

"Where's your *real* world?"

Suddenly she was Lisa again, and her smile almost made him forget his situation.

"Wherever you are, Eddie."

He realized that despite all her changes in appearance she was still holding his hand, so he pulled her toward him, leaned down, and kissed her.

"At least *you're* not an illusion," he said.

"I never was," she replied.

"And that was really you in Casablanca and Camelot and the other places?"

She nodded. "It was really me."

"Why didn't you tell me?"

"It would have been against the rules," said Lisa.

"Rules?" he repeated. "*What* rules?"

"The ones that I live by, that govern me."

"But the rules say you can tell me all this when we're in the real world—*my* real world?"

"No, Eddie."

"But you just told me!" he said, frowning.

"I know."

"Well, then?"

"I broke my rules, Eddie," she said. "I did it when I spotted Mako's killer. After what I said, I didn't think you would be able to buy that I was just Lisa and no one else." She smiled a bittersweet smile. "Perhaps I was wrong."

"What will happen to you for breaking your rules?" he asked.

"Nothing, until we know how this adventure ends."

"Adventure?" he repeated. "You mean in Manhattan?"

"No, Eddie."

"This is the beginning of something else, like being an African hunter or a Frankensteinian monster?"

"No, Eddie. The episode in question is your life."

"My life?" he repeated with a confused frown.

"You must know by now that it's not a normal life," said Lisa.

"You make it sound like it's not a *real* life at all," he said, "like I'm some kind of puppet who's being Eddie Raven this week and will be someone else next month." He grimaced. "But I've been doing that since you and Mako and Rofocale were shot, and I always wind up as Eddie Raven." He stared intently at her. "So *am* I me—I mean Raven—or not?"

She stared into his eyes. "It's a real life, and you're Eddie Raven." Then she paused and added, "At the very least."

"I'd ask you to explain, but somehow I know you'd just give me a bullshit answer that would be more confusing than no answer at all."

"I'm sorry you feel that way, Eddie," she said.

"*You're* sorry?" he said with a bitter laugh.

"Eddie, I wouldn't be breaking the rules and jeopardizing my safety if I didn't care for you—and more to the point, *believe* in you."

He sighed and hugged her. "I know I'm being difficult tonight, but that answer makes it all okay," he said, then released her and shrugged. "Well, ninety percent okay, anyway."

"Just remember, Eddie," she said. "Whatever happens, I'm on your side."

"That means a lot," he said. He glanced briefly at the kitchen. "I've been gone so long I think just about everything I have to eat is spoiled. Would you like to go out for a meal?"

But as he turned back, he found that he was speaking to an empty room.

10

Okay, what now? he wondered. *What else have you got in mind for me? And more to the point, what are you preparing me for?*

There was no answer, of course.

"Well, what the hell," he muttered. "I'm pretty sure I'm Eddie Raven, but I'm not sure of a hell of a lot else. I may only know two people in this Manhattan, this universe, and one of them just vanished. I suppose I might as well try to connect with the other, even though if I were a betting man I'd give odds against it."

He opened the door, remembered to lock it behind him (unlike the last few times), and was soon out on the street, walking toward Rofocale's dilapidated building and even more dilapidated room.

"Hey, fella," said a voice from the shadows. "You need a little protection?"

"That's a new pitch," said Raven.

"But an earnest one."

"Who are you protecting me against?" asked Raven.

The speaker, all seven feet and four hundred pounds of him, stepped out from between two buildings. *"Me,"* he said with a smile that implied he'd be just as happy, perhaps even more so, if Raven turned down his offer.

Not to worry, Eddie, whispered Lisa's voice in his ear. *He's just a cheap crook, not one of them.*

One of whom? thought Raven.

Just trust me. You have nothing to fear from him.

Right, thought Raven sardonically. *He only outweighs me by a couple of hundred pounds, all of it muscle.*

You've faced worse, Frankie. Or should I say Alan? Or Mordred?

"I'm waiting for an answer, Mac," said the huge man.

"It's still a pleasant night," replied Raven.

The man frowned. "What the hell does that have to do with anything?"

"Since I don't plan to pay you until Hell freezes over, it means you showed up a few years too early. Now get the hell out of my way before I get really annoyed with you."

The huge man sneered at him. "Okay, fella—you asked for it!"

He had time to shoot one quick thought off at Lisa—*I hope to hell you're right!*—and then the man was upon him, raining blows right and left. But with a speed he didn't know he possessed, Raven ducked most of them and blocked the rest. He backed up a few feet as the man kept coming after him, and managed to get in two quick punches—one bloodied the man's nose and the other shut his left eye.

The man stopped swinging long enough to press a hand against his swollen eye.

"Who the hell *are* you, anyway?" he demanded.

"Someone who doesn't like to be threatened or attacked by dumb palookas," answered Raven. "And I'll tell you something else: There are a hell of a lot of us walking the streets after dark, just waiting to teach bastards like you a lesson. So if you've got half a brain, and based on the last few minutes that's being generous, you'll find a better way to make a living before one of us gets really mad at you."

The huge man stared at him. Raven thought for a moment that he was going to extend a hand in friendship. Instead he spat on the street, pulled out a handkerchief, blew his nose, turning the entire fabric red, and retreated to his hiding place between buildings.

Thanks, thought Raven.

What for? asked Lisa.

For your help.

I didn't help you, Eddie.

I'm not that strong or that fast.

You'd be surprised at what you are, Eddie.

Okay, he thought. *What am I?*

He could almost see her smiling as she answered him. *That would be telling.*

And there's some rule against telling me?

I know you think there isn't, or shouldn't be, but remember: I am the Mistress of Illusions. I operate under a different set of . . . well, rules, ethics, principles, whatever you want to call them. There was a pause. *Anyway, I'm glad you faced up to the danger.*

Let me guess, thought Raven. *This was a test?*

Not a planned or predetermined one, no, she replied, *but a test nonetheless—and it was essential that you pass it, for greater tests lie ahead. Far greater.*

I don't suppose you'd care to enlighten me about them, or why I have to take them at all?

He could almost see and hear her chuckle. *Right the first time.*

Then, if you don't mind, I'll be on my way before I face any more tests by guys who are too big to play defensive end for the Giants or the Patriots.

He waited for an answer, and when none came, he examined the contours of his mind and found that she was no longer in contact with it.

He resumed walking, stopped at an all-night eatery for a sandwich, a piece of pie, and a cup of coffee, tried without much success to make sense of the day's events, and finally left a couple of dollars on the counter, got up, and began walking again.

What the hell is going on? he wondered for the hundredth time. *What did the Master of Dreams, whoever he was, have against me? Why has the Mistress of Illusions made me her special project, or even her boyfriend? Why is Lucifer's right-hand man—or right-hand demon—actually trying to help me? I keep trying to go back over my life, pulling up meaningful incidents, but Rofocale took most of it away from me. I think I was a normal guy, I feel like one, but who the hell knows?*

Damn it all! I've already had a demonstration of how Rofocale can tamper with my memory. So what is the truth?

And the only truth he could be sure of was that he didn't know.

11

He wandered aimlessly for a few blocks, realized that such behavior in Manhattan verged on suicidal, headed over to Rofocale's building, tried the door of the demon's apartment, and found it locked.

Well, at least you're walking, he thought, which was preferable to the alternatives that Rofocale could extend his arm from the bed to the door handle, or that he had died and the landlord had locked the door after disposing of the body.

Raven went back out onto the street, turned to his right, walked up to the corner, and was waiting for the light to change when he was approached by an old lady holding a batch of helium-filled balloons by their strings.

"Evening, mister," she said in a hoarse, very tired voice.

"Not interested," said Raven.

"You're not interested in evenings?" she said. "I don't blame you. I prefer sunlight."

Raven smiled. "I mean, I'm not interested in whatever you're selling."

"Without even knowing what it is?" she said. "What if it's a trip to the wildly exotic Bahamas?"

"You're not going to believe it, but I've been to more exotic places in the past couple of days. *Much* more."

"Then it's lucky for both of us that I'm not selling trips to the Bahamas, isn't it?"

"I'd have to agree," said Raven. He smiled. "And I'm still not interested."

"In what?"

"A lot of things—including balloons."

"What makes you think I'm selling balloons?" she said. "Maybe I'm selling Mitzi, my kid sister."

"Are you?" he asked, looking around.

"No. But *if* I was . . ."

"I'd politely decline," said Raven. "The light's changed twice since we started talking. Why don't you make your sales pitch, and then we can both be on our way?"

She reached into a pocket and withdrew a glowing blue marble, about the size of a wisdom tooth.

"I haven't played marbles in twenty years," said Raven.

"*I* haven't played marbles in *sixty* years," she replied. "But this isn't for playing. It's a good luck charm." She stared intently at him. "You strike me as a man who could use one."

"Oh?"

She nodded her head. "It's a very unusual charm, for very unusual dangers."

"What kind of dangers do you think I'm going to encounter?" he asked.

She smiled. "I'm just a poor saleswoman, sir, not a prognosticator."

"But you're enough of a prognosticator to know I need a good luck charm?"

She smiled again. "Not I, sir. As I said, I'm merely a sales-woman. It was the charm that selected you."

"Could you explain that, please?" said Raven.

"Probably not," she replied. "At least, not in a manner than you would accept." She looked at her naked wrist. "My good-ness, it's getting late. Please pay me and I'll be heading home."

"How much?" asked Raven.

She frowned. "What's it worth to you, good sir?"

He reached into a pocket, withdrew his wallet, pulled out a five-dollar bill, and handed it to her.

"Acceptable?" he said.

"I would have thought your life was worth more than that," she said. Then he shrugged. "But what the hell—mine isn't. Yes, we have a bargain. May it protect you in time of need." She turned away from him and began walking. "But not be-fore I get home safe and sound."

He watched her for perhaps a minute, then crossed the street. He considered the past few minutes, had a difficult time believing he had actually experienced them, and stuck a hand in his pants pocket, grasping the marble.

"Were you watching, Lisa?" he said softly as he walked down the empty street. "Was this your idea, and can you give me a hint about what the hell I'm going to need it for?"

But there was no answer.

Still restless despite the late hour, he headed toward some lights, found a small tavern open, entered, and sat down on a stool at the bar.

"What'll it be, fella?" asked the bartender.

Raven shrugged. "A beer, I guess."

The bartender walked to the tap and activated it. There

were some spurting sounds, and he frowned. Finally he pulled the half-filled glass away and carried it over to Raven.

"Ran out of beer until the five a.m. delivery," said the bartender. "No charge for less than a full glass. This is your lucky night, fella."

"Thanks," said Raven. Silently he added, *I hope it brings me better luck than that.* "I've been out of circulation for a few days—so what's new?"

"Mets lost another one. Knicks are fighting their number one pick over his salary, or their offer of his salary, or something. Anyway, it's got to do with money. Aqueduct's coming up fast tomorrow, and Can't Miss looks pretty good in the fourth race."

"Any news that doesn't concern sports?"

The bartender grimaced. "Nothing's changed. They still want to raise taxes, they still overpay everyone in the mayor's office and still underpay all the cops, they still haven't figured out how to pay for another tunnel under the East River."

"Could be worse," said Raven. "A red-tinted demon could walk in the door, looking for someone to carry off."

"Wherever he takes 'em, it can't be any worse than *here*," said a man whom Raven hadn't seen before sitting at the far end of the bar.

"Oh, I don't know," said another man who was seated alone at a small table in a corner. "Hard to believe that Hell isn't a *little* bit worse." He paused. "'Course, they ain't got no beer in Hell."

"They ain't got any here, neither," said the man at the bar.

Somehow, thought Raven, *this isn't any more interesting or enlightening that sitting alone in my apartment, staring at a wall.* He drained his glass, nodded at the bartender, then walked to the door and out into the street.

He looked at the sky, hopeful for a sign of impending daylight but seeing none.

All right, he thought. *I don't know what the hell I'm looking for anyway. Am I glad to be back? Kind of. Nothing wrong with being Alan Quatermain or Fitzwilliam Darcy, though I can think of lots of people I'd rather be than Frankenstein's monster, if he's a people at all.* He frowned. *How can she just tell me she's the Mistress of Illusions and then vanish?*

He grimaced, reached for a cigarette, suddenly remembered that he didn't smoke, and increased his pace. There was a drunk sprawled across the sidewalk, and he stepped around, rather than over, him.

He stopped mid-block, looking back the way he had come, then the direction in which he was going, and finally at the dilapidated buildings that seemed to be surrounding him and closing in upon him.

"Back off!" he muttered softly enough that no one lingering between the buildings could hear him. "I may not be the Master of Dreams or the Mistress of Illusions, but I'm somebody pretty damned important or I wouldn't even know them, so keep your distance."

There was no response, nor had he really anticipated any.

He decided he'd experienced enough strangeness for one night, decided to put off seeing Rofocale until tomorrow, increased his pace, walked the last few blocks to his apartment building, opened the front door, climbed the stairs to his apartment, pulled out his key, and unlocked the door. Before he entered, he reached his right hand into his pants pocket and clutched the marble, then let go of it after he'd turned on the lights and convinced himself that the apartment was empty.

He considered turning on the television, decided that there was nothing that he cared to see two hours before dawn, and considered sitting down with a good book, which required him to walk over to his bookcase and select one.

He was confronted by short rows of mystery, adventure, and science fiction books, plus a couple of mainstream paperbacks, and even a biography or two.

So what'll it be? he asked himself.

"So what'll it be?" said a harsh voice.

Was that me?

"Damn it, speak up!" said the voice. "I ain't got all day, Robin!"

He looked around, but the familiar walls and furnishings of his apartment had vanished. He was in a stone-walled room, with sturdy metal bars on the door and windows. He looked down and saw he was wearing some kind of outfit made of a very coarse cloth that exposed his arms and most of his legs. Standing next to him was a blond man who bore the physique of a defensive end, close to seven feet tall and three hundred pounds, and dressed in much the same manner.

"I'm asking one last time," said the voice from the other side of the door, "and if I don't get an answer, you can do without anything to eat until tomorrow."

"We'll take the goat," said his companion.

"Okay," said the man. "And remember, Little John, you've got a cellmate now, so leave the poor bastard a bite or two."

Little John cursed at him and spat on the filthy floor.

"As if we had a choice," he said to Raven. "We could have goat, or we could have goat."

"How long have we been here?" asked Raven.

Little John stared at him and shook his head. "They really busted your noggin, didn't they, Robin? I've been here maybe three weeks. They just dragged you in four or five hours ago."

"Where is 'here'?" asked Raven.

"I guess you could call it the Sheriff of Nottingham's hotel for enemies." Suddenly Little John smiled. "And he ain't got no greater enemies than Robin Hood and his Merry Men."

12

*T*hanks *a heap, Rofocale,* he thought bitterly. *Or was it you, Lisa?*

There were no answering thoughts.

He examined his surroundings more thoroughly. A snuffed candle was in a rusted holder on the wall. He assumed they lit it at night, but since he'd yet to spend a night here, he didn't know for sure. There were no beds or cots, just two piles of torn blankets that passed for beds. There was no bathroom, of course, but he noticed that Little John avoided the farthest corner of the cell, and he decided to avoid it as well.

There was nothing to read, nor anything to eat or drink, not even a pitcher of water.

He walked over to the door and examined the lock. It looked like it was completely rusted, but when he tried to maneuver the door he found that it was still held firmly in place.

Finally he sat down on the cracked stone floor and propped his back up against a filthy wall.

"I could have told you that the cell's secure," said Little John, "but being Robin, I knew you'd check it out for yourself."

"How did they capture you?" asked Raven.

"Just clumsy," said Little John. "You may have noticed that there's not a decent cook among all the Merry Men, so one night I sneaked into Nottingham, found the baker's hut, and grabbed a pot filled with roasted pig." He smiled at the memory of it. "It smelled heavenly, Robin." Suddenly he frowned. "I was just leaving with it when I tripped over some pans on the floor. Made almost enough clatter to wake all the soldiers we've already killed. So I walked out the door and half a dozen of the sheriff's men were waiting for me." He grimaced. "I did all right. Killed four of them before replacements arrived, but eventually their sheer weight of numbers overwhelmed me, and I woke up, all torn and bleeding, in this beautiful guest accommodation."

"And no one's tried to rescue you?" asked Raven.

"I don't think Friar Tuck and the rest know where I am, or even that I'm still alive," answered Little John. Suddenly he smiled. "But now you're missing too, so you can be sure they'll be sending out search parties."

"How well guarded is this place?"

Little John shrugged. "I don't even know *where* it is, let alone how well guarded. My guess is that it's off the beaten track, since otherwise they'd post a hundred guards with a prisoner like Robin Hood in their possession, and all that would do is tell the Merry Men where to look for you."

"I hate to admit it, but that makes sense," replied Raven. He paused. "So I guess we'll have to break out on our own."

"I'm open to suggestions," said Little John without much enthusiasm. "Do we tear down the door, break through a wall, or pull all the bars out of the window?"

"We consider all the possibilities and choose the one most

likely to succeed," answered Raven. "Or least likely to fail, which comes to the same thing."

"How are things on the outside?" asked Little John. "I figure I've been here a couple of weeks."

"I have no idea."

"What are you talking about?"

"It's a long story," said Raven. *And one that would be impossible for an illiterate medieval outlaw to believe,* he added mentally.

"Ah, well, wherever you were, I hope the sheriff is considerably the poorer for it—either in treasure or men, or, better still, both."

"How often do they feed us?" asked Raven.

"Three meals a day," said Little John. Suddenly he grinned. "Well, one meal a week, actually, spread over twenty-one servings."

"Sounds about right. We got any water, or is that rationed too?"

"Rationed, no. Filthy, yes," said Little John, pointing to a rusty bucket just to the left of the prison door.

"Any other prisoners here?" asked Raven.

"Almost certainly, though I suspect none of them stay for long. You can hear the screams from what passes for the courtyard every morning. I think you and I are the only ones who are here permanently. He's got information to torture out of us before he kills us."

Somehow I intuit that you're one of the optimists, thought Raven. *Now, that's really depressing.*

Don't give up hope, said Rofocale's voice inside his head. *Great challenges await you.*

It sounds like one of them will be living to lunchtime, and the greatest will be surviving all the way to next week.

Adjust your attitude, Eddie. We need you.

I'm trying, goddamn you!

Raven was about to shoot another thought across time and space when Little John nudged him with a knee.

"Company," he said softly.

"Oh?"

"Suddenly we're the most popular place in town."

They could hear the key inserted into the lock, the door squeaked open, and a bruised and bloodied prisoner was shoved into the cell.

"Welcome to our humble abode," said Little John. He stared intently at the man. "Do we know you?"

"Not if you're Robin Hood and Little John like the guards said," answered the man. "I'm just a farmer from across the river."

"What was your particular crime?"

"I've been supplying meat for the sheriff's men. Today they came by and demanded my last fifteen pigs."

"And you refused?" asked Raven.

"I only had fourteen. My family had eaten the fifteenth two days ago—so they arrested me." He shook his head sadly. "I wonder what will become of my wife and children now?"

"You'll find out before too long," said Little John soothingly.

"How?" asked the distraught farmer.

Little John jerked a thumb in Raven's direction. "This is Robin Hood. The Merry Men aren't going to let him rot here.

They're probably on their way to break him out even as we speak."

"You really think so?" said the farmer.

"You have my word on it," said Little John, turning to face the farmer, so that only Raven could see his fingers crossed behind his back.

13

"All right," said Raven after he and Little John had made their cellmate as comfortable as possible. "How many guards come by to feed us, or clean us, or whatever they hell they do?"

"*Clean* us?" said Little John, throwing back his head and laughing.

"All right, feed us," Raven corrected himself.

"Usually a pair of them, but that's when I was alone in the cell. We'll get at least two, probably three or four with you and the farmer here now." He paused. "And maybe a couple of dozen of them if they've figured out who you are."

"Let's assume three or four," said Raven.

"Okay, let's assume," replied Little John. "None of us has any weapons, none of us has any armor, and my guess is that our new friend here has never killed anything more dangerous than a chicken or a calf."

"That's not so!" snapped the farmer. "Every now and then I slaughter a full-grown cow."

"That makes all the difference," said Little John with a smile.

"All right," said Raven. "Three or four, all armed. Any armor?"

"Not usually," answered Little John. "After all, they're the captors and this is their stronghold. And hell, if we actually break out of the cell, we probably have to make our way past a hundred of them before we're out of the goddamned building."

"We'll worry about that when we come to them," said Raven. "First things first: We have to get out of the cell."

"We'll be two unarmed men up against four armed warriors," replied Little John. "I'm open to suggestions. If anyone can get us out of here, it's you."

Selling cut-rate dresses hasn't exactly prepared me for this, thought Raven wryly.

"I'm thinking on it."

"You'll come up with something. After all, you're Robin Hood."

"Let's start by assuming our new friend here isn't going to be worth anything in a fight."

"I'd call that a reasonable assumption," agreed Little John.

"Still, there's no reason why we can't put him to some use."

"How?"

"Give me your belt," said Raven, reaching for the rope around his companion's waist.

"My pants will fall down!" complained Little John.

"Come on," said Raven, staring at Little John's pants. "You have two more good meals and the damned things will split. They're not in any danger of falling down."

Little John opened his mouth to utter an argument, then

suddenly shrugged, unbuckled his belt, and handed it to Raven.

"Okay," said Raven, walking to the back wall of the cell. "Help me find something we can hang it on."

"What the hell for?" asked Little John.

"Let's find it, and then I'll show you."

The two men walked around the farmer and began examining the back wall.

"Got the remnants of a spike or a nail or something else sharp over here," said Little John, indicating a spot about seven feet above the floor.

"Loop the belt over it and see if it'll hold it," said Raven.

Little John did as he was instructed. "It'll hold if there's nothing attached to the belt, but it's not big or strong enough to hold anything much heavier than another belt."

"It won't have to," said Raven. He turned to the farmer. "You! What's your name?"

"Enoch," replied the farmer.

"Okay, Enoch. Little John and I will be escaping sometime today. May I assume you'd like to come with us?"

Enoch nodded his head. "Given the alternative," he said.

"Okay," said Raven. "Go sit against a wall and relax." He turned to Little John. "You, too."

"That's *it*?" said Little John. "You're all through planning our escape?"

"Unless you know a way to contact Friar Tuck and the rest of the band, that's it," said Raven, sitting down near the door, where he hoped he'd be able to hear men approaching.

They sat in silence for another ten minutes, and then Raven

did indeed hear the sound of men approaching. He got to his feet, signaled Enoch to follow him, and walked to where the belt hung from the wall. He quickly removed it, looped it around Enoch's neck, backed him up to the wall, and managed to tie the end of the belt around the protrusion.

"As soon as they get here, or close to here, act like you've been strangled. Your body can't go limp because the belt will never hold, but make it *look* like you're limp. Close your eyes, let your tongue hang out and your arms hang down."

"Then what?"

"Then we hope they'll be so curious that they all gather around you, however many of them there are, and Little John and I will hopefully grab a sword or two and attack them from behind."

"That's going to take a lot of luck and an equal lot of imagination," said Little John dubiously.

"You've been here a couple of weeks," replied Raven. "Have you had a better idea?"

Little John sighed deeply. "We'll do it your way."

They heard a door open down the corridor.

"Okay, Enoch," said Raven softly. "You're dead. Little John, you're sleeping at this end of the cell, facing him." Raven himself sat down with his back against a wall, and the door between himself and Little John.

It turned out that there were only two armed guards.

"What in blazes is going on here?" demanded the first to reach the cell.

"He didn't like being imprisoned," said Raven.

"Should we summon help?" asked the second guard.

"Why bother?" replied the first. "He's obviously dead. We'll get that rope off him and cart him out of here."

"Don't let us stop you," said Raven as they unlocked the cell door.

"I heard we had a new one," said the first guard. "Just watch your tongue or you'll end up like your friend here, and sooner than you think."

The two guards walked over to cut Enoch loose, but he just collapsed in their arms since he wasn't actually attached to anything. Raven nodded to Little John, and the two of them hurled themselves at the guards from behind.

Little John's man fell with a bone-crunching *thud!*—he was well-built and well-armored, but a hundred pounds lighter than his attacker. Raven's man stumbled as Raven threw himself upon him, but regained his balance in a few seconds, turned, and faced his antagonist. A grin crossed his lips as he pulled his sword out of its scabbard. "By God, I'll become famous as the man who killed Robin Hood."

"Not in this lifetime," said Little John, plunging his fallen foe's sword into the guard who was confronting Raven. The man looked surprised, then frowned, then opened his mouth to say something—but all that came out was blood, and a moment later he collapsed to the floor.

"Thanks," said Raven. "Anytime I'm in jail from now on, I hope you're my cellmate."

"Just a second," said Little John, plunging the sword into the neck of his original foe, who lay unconscious on the floor. "I was in such a hurry to help you, I forgot to kill him." He shrugged. "Not that he was going to wake up for a few hours."

"Okay," said Raven, stepping out into the corridor and looking in both directions. "Do you know how to get the hell out of here?"

"Two directions," replied Little John. "Fifty-fifty chance whatever we choose is the right direction."

"I can make it higher than that," said Enoch, removing the belt.

"You know something we don't know?" said Raven. "Good!"

"I know that there's a room where they question prisoners, and it's got half a dozen armed men, because often they take entire families or enemy units."

"And it's this way?" said Raven, pointing off to his right.

Enoch shook his head. "It's to the left."

"But that's where the guards came from."

Enoch smiled. "But we know something the remaining guards don't know."

"Oh?" said Little John.

"We know these two are dead. They didn't have time to scream or shout."

"Why does that make a difference?"

"Because it means we won't run into one or two stray soldiers in the corridor," said Enoch. "If we're quiet, we'll walk right out past their inquiry room and their quarters."

"You clearly know something we don't know," said Raven. "Before we walk blindly into a troop of soldiers, why don't you share it with us?"

"All right," said Enoch. Suddenly he smiled. "McGillicuddy roams those corridors."

"McGillicuddy?"

Enoch nodded. "He's a leopard."

"There aren't any leopards in England," said Raven.

"The sheriff's dear friend, Sir Guy of Gisbourne, captured him as a cub on a hunting trip to Africa five years ago," replied Enoch. "Now he roams the prison at night. He knows not to attack the armed guards, but woe betide any prisoner who has the misfortune to escape from his cell."

"Interesting," said Raven. "But you don't seem especially worried."

"McGillicuddy's my friend," answered Enoch.

"Explain, please."

"He eats meat. Where do you think they get it?" Enoch tapped his chest with his thumb. "I raise the tastiest cattle in the country. And since no one quite trusts McGillicuddy, I toss him his food almost every day."

"So do you plan to toss him me or Robin?" asked Little John gruffly.

"We have the warriors' swords," answered Enoch. "Let's just cut off an arm or a leg, carry it along with us, and when McGillicuddy races up out of the darkness, as he is inclined to do, we'll toss it to him and continue on our way while he's busy eating."

Little John turned to Raven. "You know," he said, "it makes sense."

"Certainly more sense than any alternative," agreed Raven. "Chop off an arm and let's get going before they notice that the guards haven't reported back."

Little John picked up a sword and bent to his grisly task, gave the severed arm to Enoch, and a moment later the three of them entered the long, darkened corridor.

Raven couldn't believe that it was going to be this easy—or

that he had reached the point where he actually considered "easy" an applicable term, but five minutes later he had come face to face with McGillicuddy, mere seconds after that the leopard was happily chewing on its gruesome trophy, and another few minutes found the three of them walking unmolested and even unnoticed out the door and headed for the safety of Sherwood Forest.

14

"Well, look who's back!" said a loud booming voice after they were almost a mile into the thick forest.

Raven looked ahead and saw a bearded man in a dark robe and sandals standing in the middle of the trail they'd been traversing. "And you even brought Little John and a peasant with you!"

I must know him, thought Raven, *but who the hell is he?*

"I hope you have some food handy, Friar Tuck," said Little John. "We haven't eaten for days."

"Days?" asked Friar Tuck, arching an eyebrow.

"Well, hours, anyway."

"Well, we're delighted to have you back," answered Friar Tuck. "It saves us the trouble of rescuing you. Although Maid Marian was sure you could do it without our help."

"Where is she?" asked Raven, hoping that when she appeared she would actually be Lisa.

"Right here," said a familiar voice, as Lisa stepped out from between two ancient trees. "I'm glad you're back, Robin. I knew no jail could hold you."

If you're the Mistress of Illusions, thought Raven, *you prob-*

ably arranged it all—the jail, the capture, the jailbreak. I just wish I knew why.

"Hello, Marian," he said, fighting the urge to call her Lisa. "You're well, I hope?"

She smiled. "*I* haven't been cooped up in the sheriff's jail, or hunting for an exit with a leopard for a companion."

He returned her smile. "I wish I could say the same."

"Did you get a layout of the prison?" asked Friar Tuck. "Might come in handy."

"Are you planning on getting captured?" asked Little John with a laugh.

"No," said Friar Tuck. "But if we're going to invade the sheriff's stronghold, that might be the way they'll least expect us."

"Makes sense," agreed Raven.

Friar Tuck turned and began walking, the others fell into step behind him, and Raven maneuvered until he was walking alongside Maid Marian.

"You're Lisa, right?" he whispered.

"You know who I am," she answered softly.

"What the hell are we doing here?" he asked.

"Staying free and planning to overthrow the Sheriff of Nottingham, of course."

"I mean *us*," said Raven. "As in you and me."

"It's all preparation," she said.

"For *what*?"

She gave him a mysterious smile. "For what lies ahead for you, of course."

"For *me*, not for *us*?"

"Don't ask too many questions, Eddie. It'll just make your head hurt."

"You called me Eddie."

She sighed. "It was a mistake. I shouldn't have."

"Where are we going?"

"I hate to use the word 'hideout,'" she said. "Let's say that we're going to our sanctuary."

"And nobody's objected?"

"Why should they? You're Robin Hood."

"But you're not part of this milieu," said Raven. "You're here because of me."

She smiled. "How do you know you're not here because of *me*?" she replied. "After all, I *am* the Mistress of Illusions."

Raven exhaled deeply. "I hate to ask it, but if you really are the Mistress of Illusions, and after the last couple of months I have no reason to doubt it, why do you even have an interest in a normal, everyday, totally unexceptional guy like me?"

She stared into his eyes. "Because you're *much* more than that, Eddie. Entire worlds depend on you. Haven't you figured that out yet?"

"I keep getting tossed into them," he answered, "but I sure as hell haven't seen anything depending on me."

The trace of a smile played across her lips. "To put it in your vernacular, Eddie, this is spring training."

"For *what*?" he insisted.

"For what lies ahead," she answered, and increased her pace.

Suddenly two men stepped out of the heavy cover and blocked their path. Raven turned questioningly to Lisa.

"Will Scarlet and Alan-a-Dale," she whispered. "They're on our side."

The group came to a halt, and Will Scarlet, tall, lean, deeply sun-bronzed, stepped forward.

"Been looking for you," he said directly to Raven. "Word has reached us that the sheriff is really enraged that you escaped his prison, and he's sent out a troop of sixty men to find and kill you." He paused. "Well, you and Little John and the peasant, but I assume he means all of us."

"What are we going to do?" asked Friar Tuck.

"We can't outmuscle them," answered Lisa, "so we'll have to outsmart them."

"Fine," said Raven. "How?"

Think, Eddie, came the thought from Lisa. *You weren't the biggest dress merchant, or the best, but you always managed to make ends meet and come out ahead.*

And as he concentrated on her message, a notion began taking shape.

"Give me half a minute," he said, closing his eyes and concentrating.

The rest of the Merry Men stood in absolute silence, waiting for their leader to make his pronouncement.

Finally Raven looked up. "What's the one thing the soldiers will expect?" he said.

"That we'll be waiting for them in heavy cover," said Little John.

"Makes the most sense," agreed Friar Tuck.

"I know," said Raven. "That's why we're not going to do it. They probably have half a dozen methods of penetrating the forest and getting to us, and if they need more men they can always get them."

"Then what do you plan to do?" asked Alan-a-Dale.

Raven smiled. "They're going to be protecting their men, and their position, and every inch of the forest that they penetrate." He paused. "So what's the one thing they *won't* be protecting with their full force?"

They all stared at him, frowning.

"What if I were to tell you that if we succeed, we can probably double our number and present a true challenge to the sheriff?"

Suddenly Lisa smiled. "Oh, of course!"

The others just kept staring in puzzlement.

"The prison!" cried Raven. "While they're throwing most of their resources into the forest, we'll capture the prison, and I'm sure just about every prisoner will be more than happy to join us in exchange for his freedom."

"You know," said Friar Tuck, "it makes sense!"

"I *like* it!" said Little John.

"Quick, kill some small animal first," said Lisa.

"For practice?" asked Little John sardonically.

"For McGillicuddy," she answered.

"Damn me, she's right!" shouted Little John.

"Enoch, get your ass over here!" yelled Friar Tuck.

"I ain't going back into that prison!" growled Enoch the peasant.

"Okay, stay here alone—and good luck to you."

Enoch stepped forward. "Okay," he grumbled. "I'm with you."

"Which way are they coming?" asked Raven.

"South and southwest," answered Will Scarlet.

Raven turned to Lisa. "I don't know where I am, I don't

know where the prison is, I don't know one direction from another. What do I do?"

She smiled at him. "The answer is obvious."

And suddenly it was.

"Little John," he announced, "you spent longer in that prison than any of us. I think you should have the honor of leading us to its downfall."

"With great pride and pleasure!" roared Little John. "Follow me!"

And with that he headed off in what Raven assumed was the direction of the prison, or more explicitly, in such a manner that there was no chance they would run into any stragglers from the prison approaching from the south or southwest.

Raven and Lisa fell into step behind the rest of their troops, and made their way through the forest in relative silence.

"You think this'll work?" he asked her softly.

"Of course it will work," she said.

"I don't know," he said. "I'm putting a lot of lives at risk, lives that trust in me."

"It will work," she insisted. "Not because you're Robin Hood, but because you're Eddie Raven. Or at least, that's what we're calling you now."

"We?"

"Me, Rofocale, some others you may have briefly met and will certainly encounter again in the future."

"I wish I knew what the hell this is all about," muttered Raven.

"Telling you now wouldn't help at all," she replied. "When the time comes, you'll know—and you'll know without anyone having to tell you anything."

He stopped walking and stared at her.

"What's the matter?" she asked.

"You're frightening me."

"You're misinterpreting your emotions," said Lisa. "Eddie Raven can't be frightened."

"The hell I can't."

"Hey, come on, Robin!" yelled Alan-a-Dale. "Or there won't be any of these bastards left for you to kill."

Raven increased his pace, and soon caught up with the rest of the Merry Men. A few moments later they broke cover and found themselves facing the huge stone prison.

"Where's the town?" Raven whispered to Lisa. "All I see is the jail."

"Beyond the next hill," she said. "They didn't want it too close to the populace."

"So, Robin," said Friar Tuck, "do we take it now?"

"Why not?" said Raven, still unused to giving orders.

"Okay," said Little John. "You all heard Robin. Now, no battle cries, no screams of any kind. We want to be at the castle before the sheriff's men know we're there."

He waved his sword and began running toward the prison, and all of the Merry Men fell into step behind him.

"You should be proud, Eddie," said Lisa. "They're charging it on your say-so."

"Somehow I felt safer as a Munchkin," admitted Raven.

"You'll get over it," she replied. "If there's one person who should feel unsafe now, it's the sheriff."

The first of their men broke down the door, and suddenly there were shouts, screams, and the clanging of swords.

"I keep thinking I'm going to blink my eyes, and when I

open them I'll be back in the Garment District, and everything I think has happened since then will have been a dream."

"Ask *them* if this is a dream," she said, pointing to one of their men and two of the prison guards writhing on the ground, blood spurting from their wounds.

Raven broke into a run and reached the door, followed closely by Lisa, just as the bulk of the prison guards and warriors came racing back from the forest.

"Lock the door!" shouted Friar Tuck.

Raven shook his head. "Waste of time. *We* broke it down. Surely *they* can do so too." He looked around. "Quick! Check the closest rooms. Find some trash and bring it here."

Just under a minute later, as the returning guards were almost upon them, Raven had piled the trash to fill up the doorway, and set fire to it just before the guards could pass through it.

"Good thinking, Robin!" cried Will Scarlet. "I hope to hell there's another way out of here, so we don't have to fight our way back through the whole damned contingent of them."

"Beats the hell out of me," answered Raven. "Hunt up Enoch and ask him—and while I'm thinking of it, watch out for that damned leopard."

"Not to worry," came Little John's voice from down the main corridor. "He's happily chewing on his lunch."

"Okay," said Raven. "Little John, you, Will, and half a dozen others, stay here and guard the entrance. Anybody who knows anything about locksmithing or lock-picking, start going up and down the cell rows letting every prisoner out."

"Even if they're loyal to King John and the sheriff?" asked Alan-a-Dale.

"They're locked away in what you call a prison and I'd call a dungeon!" snapped Raven. "How the hell loyal can they be?"

"Right," said Alan-a-Dale, signaling half a dozen men to follow him as he went into the interior of the building.

"Tuck!" said Raven.

"Yes, Robin?"

"This can't be the only way in and out of this damned building. Take some men and start hunting up other means of ingress. When you find them, booby-trap them as best you can."

Friar Tuck frowned. "Booby-trap?" he repeated.

"Find ways—very painful, even fatal ways—to prevent the guards, and probably the army by now, from entering the prison."

"Ah!" said Friar Tuck with a grin. "I understand. You just used a term I'd never heard before." He signaled to the closest half-dozen men. "Follow me!"—and a moment later all six were racing down the nearest cell block.

Raven turned to Lisa. "This may work for an hour, or an afternoon, or even all through the night, but there's no way we can hold off the whole damned army, and that's surely what the sheriff's going to send once he learns what's been going on."

"Then you'll just have to think of something, won't you?" she said calmly.

"None of this bothers you," he said, frowning.

"As I said, you're being tested," replied Lisa. "It will bother me if you fail."

"It'll do more than bother you," he shot back. "It'll kill the pair of us. If you've got any ideas, any powers I'm not aware of, anything at all, this would be a good time to share them with me."

She offered him a bittersweet smile. "*I'm* not the one who's being tested, Eddie."

"But you *can* be killed, can't you?"

"Under some circumstances," she said noncommittally.

"But not these?" he persisted.

"I didn't say that," replied Lisa.

"But you meant it?"

"You're concentrating on the wrong things, Eddie," she said. "First of all, *you* have to survive. Second, your men are depending on you. You can't let them down."

He stared at her for a moment. Then a scream of agony from one of the corridors permeated the area and brought his attention back to the situation at hand.

"All right," he muttered. "Let's get this show on the road."

He began walking in the direction of the scream, and found Will Scarlet and three of his men standing over the corpses of another of his men and a prison guard.

"Have we released all the prisoners?" asked Raven.

"I think so," said Will. "All we could find, anyway."

"Has anyone seen the leopard?"

"He's not far away," answered Will. "The scream attracted his attention, and the smell of blood has kept him here."

"Okay," said Raven. "Leave the corpse here, and let the leopard get to him. It'll keep him busy for fifteen or twenty minutes, and at least we'll know where he is."

"The guards will kill him when they come back," noted Will.

"Maybe," agreed Raven. "I suppose it all depends on how fast he eats."

Will looked in the direction of the door through which they had all entered. "If we survive this, I hope to hell I'm not sharing a blanket with it when it's all over."

"A reasonable ambition," said Raven, starting to walk deeper into the interior of the jail. "How many men do you suppose work here?"

"They don't need more than about thirty," answered Will, "but part of the army is stationed here. I would imagine the total is close to one hundred."

"And we're sixty at best, probably a little less, and certainly not as well armed and armored for a battle inside the building," said Raven. "Once we free all the prisoners, we've got to get back outside and take a defensive position before they break in, someplace where our arrows will be effective. I don't think half a dozen of us were wearing any armor. The one thing we don't want is a massive swordfight." He paused. "Is there a back entrance?"

"Yes," said Tuck.

"All right. Run ahead, tell Little John, Will, and the rest to gather by it. We'll leave the building that way and take up positions for the battle to come."

"Right," said Tuck, running off down a corridor.

"That's always assuming they haven't surrounded and breached it, of course," he remarked wryly to Lisa.

"If they have," she replied, "you'll find an alternative."

He stared at her. "Are you the Mistress of Illusions or the Mistress of Outright Fantasy?"

She smiled. "Think of all you've been through, Eddie—and yet you're still here."

He grimaced. "She says, as we're surrounded and out-gunned in the middle of a medieval prison."

"I know you have your doubts, Eddie," she said. "But you weren't selected at random."

"If we survive the next hour, and I figure the odds are ten-to-one against it, I want to know how I was selected, and by whom, and for what?"

"Concentrate on the next hour first," said Lisa.

Raven took her hand and began walking toward what he assumed was the back of the jail building. When he saw a crowd of his men he approached them.

"What's the problem?" he asked. "I told you to go outside and establish positions."

"There are maybe thirty of them right outside," said Friar Tuck. "They know they can't come in while we're here by the door, but by the same token we can't go out."

Alan-a-Dale sprinted up to the group from a different corridor. "Same situation at the front," he announced. "It's a standoff."

"That can't last," said Raven. "They'll send for more men—and my guess is that we don't have enough food to hold out for any length of time." He turned to Little John. "Is the roof flat?"

"Gently sloped," was the answer.

"That'll do," said Raven.

"Robin, you're not seriously going to pour boiling liquid down on them!" said Friar Tuck. "Hell, they'll just step back and laugh at us."

"We fight with arrows, not liquids," answered Raven. "And

from what I see, they fight with swords. Now who has the advantage when we're twenty feet above the ground and they're on it?"

Friar Tuck's eyes widened. "What are we waiting for?"

Raven smiled. "For someone to suggest dragging some furniture to the doorway and setting fire to it, since it will be very difficult for our rooftop archers to hit any targets inside the building."

"You heard him!" yelled Friar Tuck. "Drag chairs, beds, anything that can burn, to the various doors and set fire to it!"

The men scurried around the building, doing as Friar Tuck had ordered, and Raven looked around for a stairway. It didn't take long to find one, and he and Lisa were soon standing on the roof, peeking unseen over the edge.

"It's going to be a slaughter," he said. "I'd feel sorry for them, if they weren't planning to kill every last one of us."

"There are two ways to end a battle to the death," said Lisa. "I prefer yours."

He smiled at her. "You know, I could really grow fond of you, especially if you'd stop leading me into one fatal situation after another."

She returned his smile. "You *can* be killed," she said. "But you're Eddie Raven, at least for the moment, so I know that you *won't* be killed." She paused. "Well, unless you're careless or foolish."

"Or mortal," he said.

"Oh, you're mortal, all right," she assured him. "That's why you have to be so careful. Important things lie ahead of you."

"And surviving the next few hours isn't important?"

"It's important to you," she said. "And to me," she added.

"But not in Nature's scheme of things?"

"Stop, Eddie," she said. "You must know that's not true. But you also know there are things I can't tell you yet."

There was a commotion as Little John and a dozen others reached the roof, followed within a couple of minutes by the rest of the Merry Men.

"You'd better take your positions and start letting those arrows fly," said Raven. "The fires can't burn in the doorways all day."

The men spread out across the gently sloped roof, and at a signal from Friar Tuck they let loose their first barrage of arrows. There were screams and curses coming up from the ground, and Raven stepped a little closer to the roof's edge to observe the carnage.

"They're up there!" cried one of the jailers, pointing to the roof.

He pulled a hatchet out of his belt and hurled it, but it had lost almost all its force by the time it reached the roof, and didn't come within ten feet of the closest potential target. Others on the ground tried the same strategy, and got nothing for their effort except a barrage of arrows.

"I guess it's working," remarked Raven to Lisa.

"I guess it is."

"Well, they should have the brains to retreat pretty soon," he said. "It's better than the alternative."

"By the time they do, you'll have lowered the odds for your men, perhaps evened them."

"You think so?"

"Free will isn't the commodity that it becomes in a few centuries, Eddie," replied Lisa. "Their job is to stay here and try to subdue or kill your men. They'll do it until they're facing absolute, unequivocal defeat and death, and maybe beyond it."

"It's going to be a bloody sight," said Raven with a grimace.

"Fortunately you won't have to see it," she said.

And suddenly he felt a disorientating sense of, not exactly motion, but displacement.

And when he opened his eyes and regained his balance, he was very definitely Elsewhere.

15

"Where the hell are we?" muttered Raven, looking around at the lush, flower-filled landscape.

"A stopover between worlds," answered Lisa, who was standing beside him. All the others had vanished—or, more precisely, had been left behind.

"Between Earth and *where*?"

She smiled and shook her head. "It's not as simple as that, Eddie."

"Somehow I'm not surprised," he answered bitterly.

"By the way, you were magnificent leading your men against the sheriff's army."

"First, I didn't so much lead them as react to the other side," said Raven. "Second, they were jailers, not soldiers. And third, they're all imaginary anyway."

She pointed to a gash on his arm that was dripping blood. "One of their swords must have had one hell of an imagination," she said.

"Okay, I was magnificent," he said. "Now where the hell are we?"

"A halfway stop."

"Halfway between *what* and *what else*?" he asked irritably.

"Between what happened last and what happens next," she answered.

He stared at her. "I love you," he said. "I hope you know that." He paused, then frowned. "But you're driving me crazy!"

"I'm sorry, Eddie," said Lisa. "Please believe me that everything you're undergoing is necessary."

"Damned well better be," he muttered. "Well, what's next?"

"I don't think you're in the right frame of mind for another excursion."

"We're calling them excursions, are we?" he said. Suddenly he shrugged. "Well, it beats calling 'em delusions." He looked around. "So we just sit here and wait for . . . for whatever?"

"No, I think you'll adjust quicker to something more familiar." She reached out. "Here, hold my hand. I don't want us to get separated, or you'll spend all your time trying to find me."

He reached out and took her hand in his. "Feels human," he remarked with a smile.

"It is," she replied. "Mostly."

He was about to ask her to qualify that last word, but suddenly the world had vanished again and they were spinning, weightless, in total darkness. After a moment his feet touched the ground, the spinning stopped, and he tightened his grip on Lisa's hand to make sure she couldn't spin off in some other direction.

He opened his eyes, not quite sure what to expect, and found himself standing beneath a streetlight on a Manhattan street. He led her to a corner and read the street sign.

"I should have known," he said. "This is Rofocale's street. His apartment is four buildings down."

"I thought as long as we were taking a break from other things, you might like to see how he's progressing," answered Lisa. "He *is* one of your sponsors."

"He's the chief demon of Hell," growled Raven.

"He's on your side," she said. "What else matters?"

"Give me a minute to come up with an answer."

"If it's a negative answer," said Lisa, "I've got another question for you."

"Oh?"

She nodded. "How can you trust the Mistress of Illusions when you can't trust the demon she clearly trusts?"

"So all the history books should know that *you* created Robin Hood and Friar Tuck and the rest?" he said dubiously.

She shook her head. "I chose the version of them in which you could function best."

He frowned. "How many versions of them are there?"

She smiled. "More than I think you can imagine."

He stared at her, tried to think of another question where the answer wouldn't confuse or frustrate him, couldn't come up with even one, then shrugged and sighed.

"Well, as long as we're here, we might as well see how he's doing."

"I intuit that he's making progress, but very slowly."

"I'll bet his boss is having a hell of a chuckle at his pain."

"Certainly not!" said Lisa.

"The Devil doesn't enjoy his lackey's pain?"

She sighed and shook her head. "You just don't understand."

"Enlighten me," said Raven.

"Eddie, even the Devil is simply a fallen angel."

He stood perfectly still for a moment. "Son of a bitch!" he muttered. "I never thought of that."

"Almost no one does," she said sadly.

"Okay, let's go check on him," said Raven, heading off to Rofocale's building with Lisa at his side.

They entered the building, walked into the elevator, found out that it wasn't working, and climbed the stairs to Rofocale's one-room apartment. Raven was about to knock when Lisa grabbed his wrist.

"It's not locked," she told him.

"You know that for a fact, do you?" he asked.

"I wouldn't say it if I didn't," she responded.

He reached out, grabbed the doorknob, twisted it, and pushed it open.

Rofocale was sitting on the edge of his bed, not looking much better than the last time Raven had seen him, but at least sitting rather than sprawled out.

"Hello, Eddie," he said. "I've been expecting you."

"You have?" said Raven, surprised.

"Ever since you returned from Sherwood."

"You knew I was there?"

"Of course," said Rofocale.

Raven stared at the red humanlike creature sitting on the bed. "You should have told me who and what you were."

"Would it have made you more comfortable in my presence?"

Raven frowned. "Probably not."

"If you took it wrong, I was in no condition to defend myself."

"I don't attack cripples," said Raven. "Not even crippled demons."

"I know," said Rofocale. "You would be He Whom We Sought if you were."

"You make it sound like a title," said Raven.

Rofocale shrugged. "In a way." He turned to Lisa. "He did as expected?"

"We wouldn't be here if he hadn't," she answered.

"Good. The time is getting close."

"The time for *what*?" demanded Raven.

"It's still a little too soon to tell you, Eddie Raven," said Rofocale. "I don't want you to be frightened or overcome by the magnitude of it."

"Of what?" persisted Raven.

"Of what we have been preparing you for," said Rofocale. He winced in discomfort. "I'd invite you to relax and visit, but this place was not created for visitors, and besides I'm sure she has more important things on tap for you. I'd accompany you, but my strength isn't up to it yet."

Ask your Dark Master for some, Raven wanted to say, but somehow he knew that if it were available Rofocale would already have it.

"All right," said Raven. "I'll check on you whenever I can."

"I appreciate your concern, but I have suffered far worse injuries over the eons, and I shall be fine."

Once I knew who and what you are, I never doubted it.

Raven held the door open for Lisa, then closed it and followed her to the stairway.

"Before we leave the building," he said, "was there anything you wanted to say to him?"

"I've already said it," she answered.

"While I was talking to him?"

She smiled. "When else?"

"You had a whole conversation with him while we were there?"

"Yes." They reached the foyer. "Don't let it distress you, Eddie. He's not a normal human being."

And neither, it would seem, is the woman I love.

She smiled again. "I read that thought. I appreciate the sentiment."

"Well," he said wryly, "I can tell that if we ever get married, one of us had damned well better not cheat."

She laughed. And then, suddenly, her face was totally serious.

"Let's survive the next few days and weeks, Eddie," she said. "Then we'll worry about getting married—if we, and the world, are still here."

"Fair enough," he agreed. "You hungry?"

"I could eat."

"I saw a Chinese restaurant about two blocks from here last time I was walking away from the apartment," said Raven. "Looked okay."

"Then let's give it a try," she replied.

"Turn left at the corner."

They walked two blocks, then turned to their right about forty feet, and entered a tastefully decorated restaurant displaying rows of fans and delicate lanterns.

"What do you think?" asked Raven.

"I think it's charming," she answered. "I hope the food is up to the décor."

A waitress approached them.

"Table for two, please," said Raven.

"Follow me, please." She turned to Lisa. "I like your outfit."

Raven looked at Lisa, blinked, shook his head, and blinked again.

"You're still Lisa?" he asked of the Asian girl in the brocaded robe who stood beside him.

"I'm still the Mistress of Illusions," she answered. "And for you, of course, I'm Lisa."

"You don't look like her."

"Adaptive coloration," she replied. "If this was a Hawaiian restaurant I might be wearing a sarong and letting my hair hang down to my waist."

"Your hair doesn't begin to reach your waist."

She smiled. "Don't bet on it, Eddie."

They continued following the waitress and a moment later were seated at a table.

They each looked at their menus, and Eddie said, "I wonder how the kung pao shrimp is."

"I'll ask," said Lisa, signaling the waitress, who returned to the table. Lisa spoke very briefly in a Chinese dialect that Raven found incomprehensible, smiled, and turned to him. "It's the specialty of the house."

"I'll have some," he said to the waitress, and Lisa ordered in the dialect. "How many languages do you speak?" he asked as the waitress retreated.

"As many as I have to," she replied.

He stared at her. "I have to ask," he continued. "Did you study them all, or do they each come naturally?"

"Yes."

"Yes what?" he persisted.

She smiled again. "Yes, one or the other."

He was sure he'd get another non-answer to anything he wanted to know, and he thought he'd go crazy indulging in idle conversation when there was so much he wanted to ask, so he sat in silence, and she accommodated him.

Finally, after almost ten minutes of silence, their meals arrived.

"Is there a way to test it?" he asked, staring at his plate.

"You think it might be too hot?" she responded.

He shook his head. "I just want to make sure it's not too deadly. If there's one thing I don't seem to be short of, it's people who want me dead."

"It's fine, Eddie. Dig in and enjoy it."

"You can tell just by looking at it?"

She smiled. "No. But Rofocale has already checked out the chef, the staff, and the kitchen."

"Just since we entered?"

"Since you suggested it as we left his building."

Raven sighed. "It's nice to have friends, even if they are demons from Hell."

"One demon, Eddie," she replied. "I am not in that category."

"Are there any other Mistresses of Illusions?" he asked.

"Not for the last . . ." She seemed to be doing the math in her head, then shrugged and smiled. "Not in a very long time."

He wanted to ask how her predecessor had died, but was afraid to have her tell him on the assumption that his enemies were probably her enemies as well.

Suddenly she leaned over and kissed him.

"What was that for?" he asked.

She smiled. "I admire your restraint. Now dig in before your food gets cold."

He took a mouthful, decided he liked it, and took another. Finally he nodded his head. "It's good," he said.

"I told you it was," replied Lisa. "You can trust me, Eddie. In fact, I'm the only person you *can* trust."

"Including Rofocale?" he asked.

"He's not a person," she answered. "And you can trust him until I tell you that you can't."

"Which will be in the far distant future, I hope?"

"I hope so, too," she said. "We'll see."

"So what's next?" asked Raven.

"Dessert."

He grimaced and shook his head. "I mean, do I become Pinocchio, or perhaps King Kong, or maybe one of the animals Noah didn't have room for on the Ark?"

"I truly don't know, Eddie," she said. "But whatever it is, I'll be there beside you, and we'll find a way to overcome it."

"Wouldn't it be easier if you and Rofocale just told me what all this is leading up to?"

An expression crossed her face that he had never seen before—apprehension? Concern? Terror?

"Okay," he said. "I'm sorry I asked."

She reached out and laid her hand on his. "I'm sorry I can't answer."

"Can't or won't?" he asked.

"In this case there's less difference between the two than I think you can imagine."

The waitress came by to pick up their plates and take their

dessert order. They waited in silence, finished their desserts in silence, and walked out the door in silence after Raven paid the bill.

"I'm sorry you're mad at me," said Lisa as they began walking down the sidewalk.

"I'm not mad," said Raven.

"But you haven't spoken in ten minutes, maybe fifteen."

A self-deprecating smile crossed his face. "I'm afraid to ask anything."

"I do not look forward to half a century of wedded silence," said Lisa.

Raven smiled. "That's the most encouraging thing I've heard in days."

She stared at him with a puzzled frown.

"That we're going to be married and live another fifty years," he explained.

"Then make sure you take care of yourself in the coming days and weeks."

"Not to worry," said Raven. "I don't plan to leave an almost-widow behind." They passed a small theater. "Assuming we survive, I wonder if they'll make a play out of it?"

"Why should they?" she asked.

"It's no more far-fetched than half the shows on Broadway," he answered. "As strange as the last few weeks have been, are they any weirder than good and bad witches, or singing bloodthirsty barbers, or bitter, mutilated men living in the depths of an opera house? How much stranger can Rofocale be?"

"I consider that a healthy attitude," said Lisa. "Ridiculous, but healthy."

He chuckled. "If we live through this, maybe we'll become

the next Burns and Allen and make everyone else laugh at this idiocy."

"That'll certainly draw anyone over the age of seventy-five or eighty," she said.

He stopped and stared at her. "But *you* know who they were. How old are you?"

"As old as my nose, and a little older than my teeth."

"That was a legitimate question."

"I'm an old-time radio fan, Eddie. There are still some of us around . . . or how did *you* know about Burns and Allen?"

"*Touché,*" he said with a wry grin.

Suddenly he felt a wind on his face. He stopped and turned to face the source of it.

"What is it, Eddie?"

He shrugged. "Just a window fan. Powerful one, though."

"Colorful, too," said Lisa.

He looked at it. Suddenly it began slowing down, and he watched in fascination as the colors—a different primary color on each blade—became more distinct.

"Pretty," commented Lisa.

"Fascinating!" said Raven.

"Come on, Eddie."

"In a minute," he said, staring at the blades.

"It's just a fan, Eddie."

He shook his head.

"I don't think so . . ." said Raven.

16

"*Oh, shit!*" muttered Raven as he adjusted himself on the large and very uncomfortable saddle.

"You're surprised?" said his companion.

Raven sighed deeply. "Shouldn't I be, Sancho?" he said. "That's a windmill, I'm astride the ugliest horse I've ever seen, you seem to be a guy, and I'm Don Quixote, all set to grab my sword or my lance and charge the damned windmill."

"Calm down, Eddie," said Lisa, reaching over and laying what she hoped was a calming hand on his arm. "*We* know you're not Don Quixote, and we know you're not about to mistake a windmill for Matagoger."

He frowned. "Matagoger?" he repeated.

"An ogre." Suddenly she smiled. "Not to worry. Don Quixote never fought it in the book either."

"I read the book in school but wasn't really into it," he admitted. "But I did see the musical, *Man of La Mancha.* Why aren't you Aldonza or Dulcinea, whichever she really was?"

"Because I think you need a full-time guide and companion," she replied. "And not to worry, I'll look like a short, mustachioed, pudgy man to anyone we encounter."

"If you're the Mistress of Illusions, why not just remain the beautiful woman you are and tinker with their minds?"

"How do you know I didn't tinker with yours instead?" she asked with an amused smile.

"Because you're a woman back in Manhattan, and in Camelot and Sherwood Forest and everywhere else I've seen you. And if my mind isn't the only one you tinkered with, I would anticipate every man we come across making a play for you."

"Well, it's good to see your brain's still working," she said.

"So what happens now?" asked Raven.

"Now we overcome whatever obstacles the Enemy throws in our way, and then return to Manhattan if we can."

"If we can?" he repeated, frowning.

"Nothing's as simple as it seems, Eddie," she said. "Not for you."

"You mentioned the Enemy," said Raven. "Who is he?"

"What makes you think it's a he?"

"Okay, who is he, she, or it?"

"The Enemy."

"You're driving me crazy!" he growled.

"Trust me, you'll know everything you need to know when you finally do need it."

"And this is another test?"

She grimaced and shook her head. "You're not testing for a role or a position, Eddie. What you are was inevitable from the start. What's happening now is that you're being prepared for what lies ahead."

"With Munchkins and white hunters and a crazy old man who goes to war with windmills?"

"When you were a Munchkin," she said, "you learned how to function in a new body, how to manipulate events so you could meet the Wizard, and even how to manipulate him. When you were Alan Quatermain you learned how to stand up to a charging carnivore that was larger than you and wanted nothing more than to kill and eat you, and how to survive in a very unfamiliar and dangerous landscape. When you were Robin Hood, you learned how to escape from bondage with no weapons or tools. When you were . . ."

"Okay, I get the picture," said Raven. "So do I wait for some new threat now?"

"You mean, stand out here in the sun, roasting in that rusty armor you're wearing?" she responded. "You can if you want, but I think it would make more sense to find the nearest village and get some food and drink." She paused, then smiled. "Unless you *want* to stand out here in the open. I think we can be reasonably sure the windmill won't attack you."

He sighed deeply. "Okay, let's be going." He tapped his ugly, underweight steed with the flat of his sword. "Come on, Secretariat."

"His name's Rocinante," said Lisa.

"Just as well," replied Raven. "Somehow he didn't strike me as a Triple Crown winner." He grimaced. "I have a feeling he'd have trouble outrunning a crippled turtle."

"He'll get you where you want to go," she said. "Or would you rather walk miles across this barren landscape in your armor during the heat of the day?"

"Bear with me," he said apologetically. "I've only been Don Quixote for maybe ninety seconds. I'm still adjusting to who and where—and *what*—I am."

"I know, Eddie," she said. "It's just that you are being tested, and it'll be difficult enough without doubting—or, worse yet, *denigrating*—who you are."

"I'm sorry," replied Raven. He looked across the bleak, barren landscape. "Okay, who attacks me next, and with what?"

"Even if I knew, I wouldn't tell you, Eddie," she said. "Remember, this is all preparation. Telling you would be like giving you the answers to an exam."

"And if I flunk the exam, I assume you have half a dozen replacements picked out?"

"No, Eddie," she said. "We don't."

"And if I decide to play hooky or drop out, then what?"

Then that's the end of everything.

He stared at her. "Your voice lost an octave or two."

"I didn't say anything, Eddie," replied Lisa.

"But—"

"That was Rofocale, Eddie."

"He's listening?" said Raven, frowning.

"Yes."

"And watching, too?"

"Are you surprised?" asked Lisa.

Raven considered it, and decided that he was annoyed as all hell, but not the least bit surprised now that he thought about it.

He grimaced again. "Still adjusting," he muttered.

They rode in silence across the flat, dusty landscape, and within about twenty minutes came to a small wooded area surrounding a small pond. There was a ramshackle building in among the trees, and he turned to Lisa. "A bar?"

"Better still," she said. "An inn, in case we don't want to

travel all through the night. And I'd hardly call it a restaurant, but we can get a meal there as long as we're not too fussy."

"You've been here before?"

"Kind of."

He stared at her, was about to ask what she meant, decided whatever she answered would just confuse him, and went back to riding in silence.

The horses sensed the water and headed directly toward it. When they reached it, Raven and Lisa dismounted while they drank, then led them to a small fenced area where they unsaddled and released them.

"One question," said Raven as he and Lisa turned and began approaching the inn.

"What is it?"

"Will you look and sound like Sancho Panza to everyone in the inn, or like Lisa?"

And as the words left his mouth, she became almost a blur in front of him for a second or two, and when she came back into focus she was a short, pudgy, mustachioed man in some need of a shave and a haircut.

"Better?" she asked in a voice that seemed to fit her appearance.

"Not better at all," he replied with a smile. "But certainly safer. Though I'm almost sorry I reminded you."

She smiled. "I've looked like this to everyone but you since we got here," she answered.

"Son of a bitch!" he muttered. "Am I ever going to learn the ground rules to this idiotic game?"

"It's not a game, Eddie," she said. "And you have two choices: learn them or die."

"I'm trying."

She lay a gnarled, hairy hand on his. "I know."

He sighed, then grimaced. "Okay," he said, "let's go in and get something to drink."

"You're not hungry?"

"Let me see the condition of the food first," he replied, and they both chuckled.

They walked up to the front door, and he reached out to open it for her, but she pulled his hand back and opened it herself. "I'm your squire," she whispered.

He walked into the room, which consisted of a bar, three or four tables, and a door leading to what he assumed was the kitchen.

"A table for my master, the great Don Quixote!" hollered Lisa.

He wanted to signal her not to call any attention to themselves, but decided she knew the protocol a lot better than he did. Still, he did remember more than a decade after having to read the book in school that Don Quixote was a figure of ridicule, so he prepared himself for everything from insults to a challenge to a duel to the death.

"Ah!" said the bartender in amused tones. "A knight errant and his lackey!"

"Keep a civil tongue in your head," growled Raven.

"Or what?" demanded the bartender.

"Or it won't be in your head for long," said Raven. "Now I want a table for my squire and myself."

"Take whatever you want, O Great Knight," said the bartender, clearly amused by Raven's appearance. "Miguel!" he called to a man sitting alone at a table in the far corner of the room. "Grab the great knight's squire and lead him to a proper table."

"Don't you lay a hand on her!" snapped Raven.

"And then do the same for the blind knight."

"Blind?" demanded Raven. "What the hell are you talking about?"

"Mighty few women serve as squires," said the bartender with a chuckle, "and even fewer sport a bushy black mustache."

"I misspoke," said Raven.

"Then he's not a girl?" said Miguel with a chuckle.

"Whatever he is, keep your hands to yourself or spend the next thirty years wishing you had."

"Bold talk for a madman in rusted armor," said Miguel.

"Don't put it to the test," said Raven. "I've had a rough week."

Miguel grinned, offered a deep bow, and led the way to a table near a large window.

"That'll do," said Raven. "Now scram."

Miguel frowned. "What is 'scram'?"

"Go away."

Miguel seemed to be considering taking a swing at Raven, decided not to harass a paying customer, and walked back to his own table.

Raven was about to pull out a chair for Lisa when he felt her hand on his wrist.

"Allow me, my master," she said, pulling the chair for him.

He grimaced, nodded his thanks, and sat down. A moment later she sat down next to him.

"Well, Brave and Noble Knight, what'll it be?" asked the bartender.

"I'd really like some coffee," said Raven softly to Lisa, "but I can't ask for it, can I?"

She shook her head. "I'm afraid not," she whispered.

"Well?" demanded the bartender.

"What do you recommend?" asked Raven.

"I recommend spending your money and getting drunk beyond belief!" replied the bartender with a laugh.

"Okay," said Raven. "A glass of your best."

"My best *what*?" was the reply. "Stout, ale, wine?"

"Stout," said Raven promptly. He turned to Lisa, and lowered his voice. "It sounded closest to beer."

She smiled.

The drink arrived, Raven took a taste, made a face, and put it down on the table.

"Well?" said the bartender?

"It's wet, anyway," replied Raven with a shrug.

"You gonna pay for it, or do I have to joust you for it?"

Lisa immediately tossed a couple of coins on the table. The bartender picked them up, bit into each of them, nodded his approval, put them in his pocket, and went back to the bar.

"I'm glad one of us had some money," said Raven. He paused. "So what do we do now?"

"We wait," she replied.

"For what?"

"I don't know."

He frowned. "That doesn't make any sense."

"I'm part of the test, Eddie," she answered. "Not its creator." She looked off to her left. "Maybe this guy can help."

A small man—smaller even than Lisa—shambled across

the room to them. He was dressed in rags and had a chain collar clasped around his throat.

"He looks familiar," said Raven.

"You're kidding!" said Lisa.

"No, I mean it."

The man stopped at their table and stared at Raven. "I heard your man say that you were the famous knight-errant Don Quixote."

Raven simply stared at him.

"Well, are you?"

"If I'm that famous, why don't you recognize me without asking?" said Raven.

"I've been a galley slave for a decade," said the man. "I've heard of you, of course, but I've never seen you until today."

"Oh?" said Raven. "And what exactly have you heard?"

"Of your heroic exploits, of course."

"Name two," said Raven.

Lisa leaned over and whispered softly into his ear. "Why are you tormenting this poor man?"

"Because he's not what he claims to be," Raven whispered backed. "I'm waiting," he said aloud.

"Noble knight, please do not ignore my supplication," whined the man. "I am the unfortunate Ginés de Pasamonte, whose life began badly and has gotten worse day by day."

"And you want it to get better?" asked Raven.

"Oh, yes, noble knight!"

"Then be out of here before I get to my feet, or I'll find out just how well this sword works."

The man's eyes widened. "Surely the noble knight is kidding!" he said plaintively.

"You've got about ten seconds to find out," said Raven, pushing his chair back from the table.

Ginés de Pasamonte turned and fled, and was out of the tavern in something under seven seconds.

"What was *that* all about?" demanded Lisa.

"Surely the Mistress of Illusions knows," said Raven.

"I'm merely a participant, a player, in this test, Eddie," she said.

"Didn't you recognize him?" said Raven.

"Should I have?"

"Back in our twenty-first century, he's Gene Pastore. He owns three sports franchises around the country, and as of last April he's serving twenty-five to life for killing his partner after he was caught robbing him."

"You know," said Lisa, "I *do* remember it. I just never paid much attention to what he looked like."

Raven looked across the room to the door leading to what he assumed was the kitchen.

"*Here's* someone who's a lot harder to forget," he said with the hint of a smile, as an absolutely gorgeous young woman approached them.

"Kind knight," said the woman, "I will not take up your valuable time. But I could not let you leave without expressing my gratitude."

"Happily accepted," said Raven. "May I ask what it is for, and from whom it is given?"

"I am Dulcinea," she replied. "And, against my will, I was betrothed to Ginés de Pasamonte in exchange for his canceling my father's debt to him. But now that you have shown him to be the coward everyone always suspected he was, I feel all bonds with him have been broken."

"Happy to have been of service," said Raven.

"Stay well, noble knight," she said, turning and walking back to the kitchen.

"She's quite beautiful," remarked Raven.

"I'm sure you're heartbroken that she didn't burst into song," said Lisa. She gestured to his stout. "You going to drink the rest of that?"

"Not if I can help it."

"Then let's be on our way," she said.

"What the hell," he said, getting to his feet. "How many more people can we meet in a run-down tavern?"

They walked out the door, retrieved their horses, and began heading very slowly west.

"So did I pass?" he asked after a couple of minutes.

"So far so good, I imagine," she replied.

"It's not over?" he said. "This test, I mean."

"If it was, we'd be back in Manhattan."

They rode westward for another couple of miles, then came to a stream, dismounted, and allowed their horses to slake their thirsts.

"Whoops!" said Lisa.

"Whoops?" he repeated, frowning.

"Company."

Raven looked ahead, and saw the sun glinting off an incredibly bright figure approaching them on horseback.

"Damn!" he muttered. "That's almost blinding."

"It's just the way the sun's hitting it."

The figure got to within one hundred yards, and suddenly Raven chuckled.

"What's so funny?" asked Lisa. "He's close to seven feet tall, and that's a hell of a lance he's carrying."

"I just remembered the book," said Raven. "He's the Knight of the Mirrors. I'm supposed to see myself—this ancient, feeble old man pretending to be a knight—and the sight brings me back to sanity . . . and just about kills me in the process."

"Halt!" cried the Knight of the Mirrors, bringing his horse to a stop when they were within ten yards.

"Greetings," said Raven. "What can I do for you?"

"Nothing," said the knight. "But I can do something for *you*."

"Oh?"

The knight nodded his plumed head and helmet. "Come closer, Don Quixote de la Mancha."

"You know my name," said Raven wryly. "How comforting."

"You think so, do you?" said the Knight of the Mirrors.

"Come closer still. I will not lay a finger—or a weapon—on you."

"I know," said Raven.

"Dismount, Don Quixote."

"Happy to," said Raven, getting off his horse.

The knight did the same, and approached Raven until they were less than three feet apart.

"It is time to learn the truth, Don Quixote. Look at the Knight of the Mirrors and tell me what you see."

Raven stared into the brilliant reflecting armor. "Ah!" he said.

"Well?" demanded the knight.

"I need a shave," said Raven. "I don't suppose I could borrow a razor from you?"

The knight screamed, either in outrage or agony or both, and suddenly both he and his horse completely vanished.

"I figure I get an A-plus for that one," said Raven to Lisa as he remounted his horse.

"Every incident prepares you for the ultimate test," she said. "Though I will admit your prior knowledge, both of the book and the criminal, eased you through this one."

"I'm not thrilled with the notion of being tested, especially given what I'm being tested *for*," he said. "But as long as they aren't any harder or more dangerous than these last few, I suppose things could be a lot worse."

"Give it thirty seconds," she said grimly. "They will be."

And as the words left her mouth, a magnificent coal-black stallion thundered up, ridden by a huge armored man.

"Halt!" he cried. "Who goes there?"

"Enough bullshit," muttered Raven. Aloud he said, "Eddie Raven. You got a problem with that?"

"Not as long as you and your squire pay tribute to cross my land," came the answer.

"It's pretty empty and pretty desolate," said Raven. "What makes it *your* land?"

"Right of possession," said the man. "Or do you plan to take it from me?"

"Not if I can avoid it," said Raven. "Now why don't you just let us pass in peace?"

"How would I make a living if I did not charge a tribute to those passing through my territory?"

"You got a deed to it, do you?" asked Raven, who was becoming more and more annoyed with Don Quixote's milieu.

"Certainly not," said the man. "I took it by the strength of my good right arm."

"Who the hell *are* you anyway?" demanded Raven irritably.

"I am the Knight of the White Moon, of course," came the answer.

"It's more gold than white this time of year," said Raven. "I don't think your claim or your name would hold up in a court of law."

"That's *it*!" thundered the Knight of the White Moon. "I challenge you to a battle to the death!"

"And I claim the right to choose the weapons we use," said Raven.

"Done!" cried the Knight.

Raven turned to Lisa. "You heard him, right?"

Lisa, still in her Sancho Panza guise, nodded her head.

"So what shall it be, ugly knight in rusted armor?" demanded the Knight of the White Moon. "Swords? Daggers? Both?"

"Neither," answered Raven. "I choose fisticuffs."

The Knight frowned. "Surely you jest!"

"Am I smiling?"

"That is unacceptable!"

Raven turned to Lisa. "The moment he pulls a weapon of any kind, ride off and spread the word to anyone who will listen that the Knight of the White Moon is a liar and a coward."

The Knight held up a hand. "Wait!" he said with a note of desperation in his voice. "I accept your terms."

"Good," said Raven. "The battle is over when one of the combatants cannot get up."

The Knight nodded his head.

"Did you box in college?" asked Lisa very softly.

"Even better," replied Raven. "I grew up on the West Side of Manhattan."

"Don't joke, Eddie."

"Am I smiling?" he replied. He turned to the knight. "Are you ready?"

"In a minute," said the knight, removing his boots.

"Good idea," said Raven, removing his boots, his helmet, and almost all his body armor except for his steel-reinforced gauntlets.

"Ready," said the knight, striking forward.

Raven watched him for a moment and very subtly nodded his approval. The man may or may not have possessed normal quickness under normal circumstances, but even with his boots off his body armor slowed him down considerably.

Raven danced around, jabbing, faking, ducking, and when he saw an opening he swung a steel-covered fist and clipped the knight on the chin, knocking the startled man to the ground. He was up in a few seconds, but was too slow and awkward to catch or connect with Raven, who danced skillfully around his opponent, and then landed another heavy blow to the jaw. The knight collapsed in a heap.

"Had enough?" asked Raven.

The knight looked puzzled. "This is a fight to the death."

"It doesn't have to be," said Raven. "Concede right now, promise no further hostilities, and we'll be on our way."

The knight looked puzzled, as if he'd never heard a similar proposition.

"You mean it, Don Quixote?"

"I do."

The knight reached out his hand. "Then take my hand in eternal friendship."

"Happy to," said Raven.

As he stretched his arm out, he wondered how they were going to get back to Manhattan, and how Rofocale was doing, and half a hundred other things.

What he wasn't prepared for was what happened next.

17

"Where the hell *are* we?" demanded Raven.

"What does it look like?" asked Lisa.

"Cold and damp," he replied. "Exactly the way it feels." He turned to his left. "Can't say much for the interior decorator. Damned place is nothing but one huge stone block after another."

He took a deep breath through his nose. "And it smells like . . . I dunno . . . like death warmed over."

"You'll get used to it," said Lisa. Then she shrugged. "Or you won't."

He stared at her. "You know," he said, "about thirty seconds ago, you were a pudgy, mustachioed sidekick, and before that you were an absolutely beautiful young woman."

"And now?" she asked.

"You really want to know?"

"Yes."

"An ugly hunchbacked dwarf."

She nodded. "It goes with my name . . . or at least the name you'll call me by while we're in this milieu."

"Let me guess," said Raven. "Igor?"

She gave him a nearly toothless smile. "Right."

"And I'm Dracula?"

"Looking like that, you'd damned well better be," she said with another smile, neither of which did anything to humanize her ugly, misshapen face.

"Okay," said Raven. "Don Quixote had a quest. Robin Hood had a challenge. What the hell has Dracula got?"

"I should think that would be obvious," said Lisa.

"Maybe to the Mistress of Illusions," said Raven. "But not to someone who's been a vampire for less than two minutes."

"Your job, plainly put, is to survive."

"Alone in this castle?" he said, frowning. "Should be a piece of cake, as long as I don't freeze to death."

She gestured for him to walk over and join her by a window, where she pointed down at the ground. Literally hundreds of townspeople carrying torches and spears were climbing the curving path that led up to the castle.

"Oh, shit!" muttered Raven. He looked around the barren chamber. "What kind of weapons do we have?"

"Dracula needs no weapons," said Lisa.

"Maybe Bram Stoker's Dracula didn't need any weapons, but Manhattan's Eddie Raven sure as hell does!" he shot back.

"Manhattan's Eddie Raven is going to have to improvise," she answered.

"Just between you and me . . ." he began.

"Who else is there?" she replied.

"Just between you and me, what possible purpose is served by me being a vampire?"

"It teaches you to adjust," she said. "We don't know what lies ahead when you're finally ready for your mission—which, I should add, is not that far off. Our job is to prepare you for it."

"And being a blood-sucking member of the undead helps make me ready?"

She shrugged. "It might. There are things even the Mistress of Illusions doesn't know."

"You could help, you know," said Raven.

"I *am* helping."

"You could have disarmed the Knight of the White Moon and saved me the trouble. I mean, hell, you're the Mistress of Illusions. You could have solved damned near every problem I've been faced with."

"To what purpose?" she shot back.

"What?" he half shouted in surprise.

"How would that have prepared you?"

"Prepared me for *what*?" he demanded.

For just a few seconds she was Lisa again, and she looked straight into his eyes. "For what you must do," she said. "And you must do it alone. That's why neither Rofocale nor I nor anyone else can help you now. We don't know what you'll be facing, just that it's of a far greater magnitude than anything you've faced so far—indeed, than *anybody* has ever faced—and you have to be ready for it, as ready as we can make you, anyway." She sighed deeply. "That's why you're not a warrior, or a sorcerer, or a hunter in *every* encounter."

"Okay," said Raven. "So what's expected of me as a vampire?"

They could suddenly hear the screams of the enraged townspeople approaching the castle, and in that instant she became Igor once again.

"I should have thought the answer to your question would be obvious," she replied. *"Survive!"*

He stared at her without answering, then looked down at the crowd again. An elderly man was being escorted to the front door, and he was instantly joined by a well-dressed young man and woman. The rest of the assemblage held back.

"That figures," said Raven.

She frowned. "You know them?"

"I don't *know* anyone," he replied. "We're all fictional, remember?"

"But you spoke as if you recognized them."

"To this extent: If I'm Dracula, then I know who they have to be, whether they're Bram Stoker's creations or not."

"And who are they?"

"The three people most closely associated with Dracula," replied Raven. "The older one's got to be Van Helsing, and the couple are Jonathan and Mina Harker." He paused and frowned. "At least she'll become Mina Harker by the end of the book, or if I let her live." A humorless smile crossed his misshapen face. "Doubtless they're here to talk sense into me."

"I'd better go greet them and escort them up here," said Lisa. "We don't want them to think anything's wrong or different."

"No," he agreed as she began hurrying toward the stone staircase. "After all, we're delighted to play host to people who want to kill us." He glanced out the window again. "You're just damned lucky I don't have a few cauldrons of boiling whatever to pour over the side of the roof."

"Don't get so taken by your role," she said. "Remember, it *is* just a role."

Suddenly he frowned. "*Stop!*" he snapped.

She froze. "What is it?"

"It's 1897. They haven't seen any of the movies."

"I don't understand, Eddie. What are you talking about?"

"I've actually read the damned book. A long time ago, to be sure, but it's coming back to me—and there's no Igor in it. Hollywood swiped him from the *Frankenstein* novel thirty or forty years later."

"Then who—?" she began, puzzled.

"Renfield," he answered. "Late fifties, built like a defensive lineman, crazy as a loon."

And instantly, in Igor's place, he was facing the Renfield that Bram Stoker had painstakingly described back in 1897.

Raven nodded his reluctant approval of her appearance. "Okay," he said. "Go greet our guests and bring them up here. And if possible, close and lock the door once they're inside the damned castle."

"Yes, Dracula," she said, scurrying down the remaining stairs and rushing up to the massive door. It took all her strength to swing the portal open enough for Van Helsing and the Harkers to pass through it. She wanted to ask for help closing and bolting it, but then she remembered what she now looked like, and she didn't want to arouse any further suspicions, so she put every ounce of strength she possessed into it and slowly, gradually swung the door shut.

"The count is awaiting you," she said to Van Helsing and the Harkers. "Please follow me."

The four of them climbed the stairs while Raven positioned himself against a library wall, rested his outstretched arms on the shelves, and waited for them. They entered the room a moment later.

"We meet again," said Van Helsing gruffly.

"You're panting," noted Raven. "Those are a lot of stairs for a used-up old man, especially one who has been traveling most of the day to get here. Sit down and relax."

Van Helsing seemed about to spit out a caustic reply, thought better of it, and seated himself on a leather chair.

"Welcome back, Jonathan," said Raven. "And this must be Mina."

He nodded a greeting to her. She glanced quickly at Harker, evidently saw some sign of approval, and nodded her greeting.

"I hope you found the trip comfortable," said Raven. "Except, of course, for the company."

"You could use pavement," she replied.

"That would just encourage visitors," answered Raven. "And speaking of visitors, to what do I owe the pleasure of this visit?"

"We have serious matters to discuss," said Van Helsing.

"You mean you haven't come here to amuse me with the latest jokes you picked up in the local tavern?" said Raven, feeling rather pleased with himself until he saw Lisa frown and quickly shake her head when no one was watching her.

Why the hell not? thought Raven. *I'm not going to drink anyone's lifeblood or kill anyone, but* they *don't know that, so why not tease the old man and pretend to lust for the young lady and otherwise act the way they would expect a villain to act?*

"You seem to have some unhappy townspeople lining the road to your castle," said Harker.

"Unhappy is an understatement," added Mina.

Raven smiled. "Is it my fault that I have indoor plumbing and they don't?"

"That's not what they seemed annoyed about," said Harker. "I think it may have something to do with your diet."

"What would they know about my diet?" Raven shot back. "I never patronize the local restaurants."

"Enough of this foolishness!" growled Van Helsing. "You're a vampire, and you've been feeding off the populace and unknowing visitors and travelers for years!"

"Have you ever heard of the science of genetics?" asked Raven.

"Of course."

"Neither of my parents, no one in my family, was a vampire," said Raven. "How does that jibe with your knowledge of genetics and inheritance?"

"It means you are every bit as much a genetic freak as the physical freak you appear to be," said Van Helsing.

"Let me ask you one more question, based on your supposed knowledge of vampires and vampirism," said Raven.

"Go ahead."

"Do you think that you and Harker together could subdue me in the next few minutes if it comes down to a physical battle?"

"You know we could not," said Van Helsing.

"Good!" said Raven. "Renfield, bring our guests some wine or whatever else they may want." Lisa headed off to what he assumed was the wine cellar, and he turned back to van Helsing. "I hope you've been enjoying our country. It still requires some civilizing and some landscaping and some governing, but it's certainly more livable than some."

"It is littered with too many graves," said Van Helsing.

"I hope you're not going to suggest that I am responsible for them all."

"Are you?"

I wish to hell I knew. "Probably not," said Raven.

"What are your future plans?" asked Van Helsing. "I know that you've asked Mr. Harker here to find you a suitable dwelling in the British countryside."

"There's more to see and do there," answered Raven.

"And drink?" asked Van Helsing.

Lisa reentered the chamber just then.

"Ah!" said Raven. "Speaking of drink, here come yours."

"You didn't answer my question," said Van Helsing.

"You noticed," said Raven. He walked over, took the tray from Lisa, and approached his three guests, allowing them to choose the bottle of wine they wanted, then poured each a glass and moved on to the next one.

"None for yourself?" asked Harker, as he set the tray down on a table.

"I don't drink . . . wine," said Raven. *Damn! It's almost worth going through all this shit to be able to utter that line!*

"You're smiling, Count," said Mina.

"A happy thought," he replied.

"Of torture and bloodshed?" asked Van Helsing.

"Only limited to people who annoy me," answered Raven, feeling that he finally had control of the conversation.

"Then we'd best get down to business," said Harker.

Raven resisted the urge to say "Shoot!" and merely stared at him.

"A South American party is interested in purchasing an authentic castle in this country," said Harker. "Since I assume you'll soon be moving to England, I was wondering if you'd be interested in entering a transaction for this place?"

"I don't know if I'll be staying in England," said Raven. *On the other hand, who knows how long I'll stay in this identity?* "But sure, I'd be happy to consider an offer."

"Including the surrounding area?" asked Harker.

"If I legally own it."

"How about the rotting corpses inside the castle?" asked Van Helsing.

Raven stared at him. "Were you always this unpleasant?"

Van Helsing shook his head. "Only since I discovered that vampires really and truly walked the Earth."

I'd love to correct you and say that actually we fly across the Earth, but you'd probably believe me.

Raven turned back to Harker. "Bring your offer in writing."

"Have you an attorney?"

"Just bring it to me."

"Yes, Count."

"So much for my business with Mr. Harker," said Raven. "Now, Mr. Van Helsing, what can I do for you, besides die a loud and agonizing death in front of you?"

"Actually, that would be quite sufficient," said Van Helsing, and Raven couldn't resist a chuckle.

"If I should feel it coming on anytime before you leave, which I trust will be soon now, I will certainly give you a few seconds' warning."

Van Helsing returned his smile. "And people say that vampires aren't thoughtful."

"Only the British side is thoughtful," said Raven.

"I've checked you out thoroughly," said Van Helsing. "You don't have any British blood."

"Well, there you have it," replied Raven.

They spoke, uncomfortably on the part of his visitors, and

when Raven gave them no further encouragement to talk, they finally got to their feet and said their farewells, with Harker promising to return in a day or two with the proposed offer, and Van Helsing hinting that he would be back when he was finally prepared to make sure there was one less vampire walking the Earth.

Lisa, in her Renfield identity, led them down the stairs and laboriously opened the massive door for them. Exhausted, she leaned against the huge portal, and as she did so, with her back to the door and facing the interior of the castle, three large men armed with spears and swords walked right in, took a brief look around, and began racing up the stone staircase.

Lisa wanted to warn Raven, but she realized that her primary duty at the moment was to close the door before anyone else could sneak in, and she threw herself into the chore.

Raven was standing alone in the now-empty chamber, studying the wine and wondering how it tasted. He picked up a bottle, held it to his lips, then made a face and put it back down.

Great, he thought. *I really am a vampire. I hope this test ends before I get so hungry or thirsty that I have to down a pint of blood.*

"So there you are!" growled a voice from the doorway.

Raven looked across the room and found himself facing the three burly men who'd entered the castle a moment earlier.

"What can I do for you gentlemen?" he asked. "And I use the word advisedly."

"You can die!" bellowed the closest one.

Raven smiled. "You're too late."

The man cursed and charged, wielding his sword above his head.

Raven backed up a few steps, realized that his foe was coming too fast, planted his feet, and prepared to meet the charge. He reached his right hand out for the swordsman's wrist, though since he was outweighed by some sixty pounds of muscle he didn't expect it to do much good—but to his surprise he had no trouble holding the arm aloft.

I wonder just how strong a vampire is . . .

He squeezed, the man screamed, and he could feel the wrist crumble into a dozen bone fragments beneath his vise-like grip. He swung his other arm, connected with his opponent's jaw, heard a loud crack, and saw the man's body fly through the air and bounce off a brick wall.

"Okay," said Raven. "Who's next?"

The two remaining men exchanged troubled glances, and then charged him simultaneously. Raven took what he thought would be a quick step to the left. Instead it was a leap that carried him some twenty feet through the air.

"*Halt!*" he shouted.

The two men froze.

"You've seen what I did to your foolhardy friend. You've been given a hint of what I can do against the pair of you. I offer you your lives, if you agree to leave the castle right now and never return."

The men frowned, stared at each other, and seemed torn by indecision.

"Let me help you make up your minds," said Raven. "I will count to ten. If you are still in the room when I reach ten, I will slay you more slowly and painfully than I hope you can imagine. The decision is yours."

Both had bolted out of the room and were racing down the stairs before he reached "Five."

Lisa entered the room a few seconds later. She saw the remains of the first swordsman and froze.

"*You* did that?" she asked.

"Yes."

"Barehanded?"

"Being a vampire has its advantages," he replied with a smile.

"Clearly," she said.

He walked to a window and stared down at the unhappy mass of peasants and warriors.

"So did I pass the test?" he asked.

18

"With flying colors," said a voice that was definitely not Lisa's or her characterization of Renfield.

Raven turned and looked at the source, and it was Rofocale, dressed in a distinctive red robe and standing beside his bed.

"Where is—?"

"Right here?" said Lisa, and he realized that she was standing just to his right, and that she looked like his Lisa again.

"How are you feeling?" he asked Rofocale.

"Better," said Rofocale. "And you?"

"Fine," said Raven. "But then, nobody shot me."

"Waste of time," said Rofocale contemptuously. "You can temporarily damage a demon, cause him great discomfort—but you cannot kill him."

Raven turned to Lisa. "Please tell me that Mistress of Illusions isn't another name or term for demon."

She smiled and laid her hand on his. "It's not, Eddie."

"It's nice to be called Eddie again."

"Don't get used to it," said Rofocale.

"Oh, shit!" muttered Raven. "Another test?"

Rofocale nodded his massive head. "You're not ready for the ultimate encounter yet. Trust me on this, Eddie Raven."

"I don't suppose I have the freedom or authority to respectfully decline any more tests?"

Rofocale smiled. "I like your attitude, Eddie. And no, that particular freedom is denied you."

Raven turned to Lisa. "And I don't suppose you can overrule him?"

"Why would I?" she answered. "We're all on the same side, Eddie."

He frowned. "I don't even know what side that is."

"You will soon enough," said Rofocale. He frowned. "You know, I was just going out for my first meal in weeks since leaving the hospital, when I intuited that your vampiric adventure was over." He paused. "It's got to be three in the morning, or thereabouts, and I'm unacquainted with New York City. Why don't you recommend a good all-night restaurant, or better still, come along and join me?"

Raven frowned. "I thought you lived here."

"The apartment?" said Rofocale. "A mere convenience. I probably hadn't used it five nights in the five years leading up to the incident at Mako's shop."

Raven glanced quickly at Lisa, who nodded her assent.

"Okay, we'll join you," he said. "But I'm going to want some answers before the meal's over."

"Fair enough," said Rofocale. "Now, where are we going?"

"Depends on what you like to eat," said Raven. "Screaming newborn babies perhaps?"

"I assume that is your notion of a joke rather than a legitimate guess."

"Let's say that I *hope* it is," replied Raven. "But after the past few weeks, I'm not as certain as I wish I was."

"Human food is fine."

"Well, my favorite dish is veal parmesan, and I love pastitso with dolmades and saganaki, but there aren't any good Italian or Greek joints around here that are open at three in the morning, so how's about some steak and eggs?"

"Fine. I can imbibe and digest just about anything."

"Okay," said Raven. "Barnaby's is an all-nighter, and it's about three blocks from here." He walked to the door, opened it for Lisa, followed her to the elevator, and kept the sliding door open for Rofocale.

"You're not even limping," noted Raven. "You were in a pretty bad way the last few times I saw you."

"I should probably answer that clean living does it," said Rofocale with an almost frightening smile. He turned to Lisa. "How did he do?"

"He passed the tests," she replied.

"With creativity, or merely with strength and courage?"

"With complete creativity," said Lisa.

"Good. More and more it looks like he is the Chosen One."

"Chosen One?" said Raven, frowning.

"Just an expression," said Rofocale. "Pay no attention to it."

"Your nose just grew six inches," said Raven.

Rofocale placed his hand on his nose and frowned. "What are you talking about, Eddie Raven?"

"Never mind."

"Not so far," she replied.

"Cut it out," said Raven.

Lisa turned to him. "I don't understand, Eddie."

"I've just put my life on the line in a bunch of crazed scenarios that most men couldn't have survived for five minutes," he said. "And you two are making it sound like I've made it through kindergarten or maybe first grade, and grad school still lies ahead."

"Actually," said Rofocale, "that's very well put, Eddie."

"Damn!" muttered Raven. "I knew you were going to say something like that."

"Don't look so grim," said the demon. "It should be a matter of great pride."

Raven merely glared at him and made no reply.

They reached the restaurant, which had clearly been built close to a century ago and had gone through many face changes, seated themselves at a table that boasted four plates, four cups, and a coffeepot, and waited for a waiter to come by.

Lisa filled Rofocale's coffee cup, and was about to do the same for Raven when he held up his hand.

"None for me," he said. "I've lost my appetite."

She stared at him for a moment, then filled her own cup, added some cream, and took a sip.

"It's really quite good, Eddie."

"I'm sure it is."

"Well, we may as well discuss his next test," said Rofocale, "before he gets so annoyed with his situation that he just gets up and walks out of here all alone."

"I wouldn't do that," said Raven. Then, after a few seconds' consideration, added, "Probably."

"What do you think of horses, Eddie?"

"I saw American Pharoah win the Belmont during his Triple Crown year," answered Raven.

"Not that kind of horse."

"What kind, then?"

Rofocale seemed at a loss for an answer, and looked across the table at Lisa.

"Cowboys' horses," she said. "Like Silver and Trigger, only the real thing."

"I suppose they're okay," said Raven. "Why?"

"They're going to be the primary form of transportation during your next test," she said. "Remember any cowboys' names from your reading?"

"Sure," said Raven. "Wyatt Earp, Doc Holliday, Billy the Kid, Will Bill Hickok, a few others."

"And any incident?" persisted Lisa.

"The Gunfight at the O.K. Corral."

"Good," said Rofocale. "We won't be dropping him cold."

"We'll be doing worse than that," said Lisa seriously.

"True," agreed Rofocale.

"What the hell are you talking about?" demanded Raven.

"You'll find out soon enough," said Rofocale.

"And I'll try to find a way to join you," said Lisa.

"So I'm going to be a gunslinger in the Wild West," said Raven. "Could be worse, I suppose."

"Not much," said Lisa, her voice thick with sympathy.

"Can you at least tell me where I'm going?"

"Yes, Eddie," she said.

"Well?"

"Tombstone."

19

He was leaning against the top of a corral, lazily watching the cattle that were enclosed by it. The desert sun beat down on him and he reached an arm up to wipe the sweat off his brow, only to find out that he was wearing what he'd been taught to call a ten-gallon Stetson when he was a kid reading cowboy comics and watching movies about the Wild West—which, he knew, was probably not anywhere near as wild as legend had it.

Except in Tombstone.

"Damned hot day, Ike," said the man standing next to him. They were similarly attired: jeans, shirt, vest, neckerchief, Stetson.

"That it is," replied Raven, wondering who he was talking to—and even more important, who he himself was.

"Your dad says the horses probably won't arrive before to-morrow," continued the young man. "Tonight at the earliest. Not much sense hanging around here in the sun."

"You got a point," agreed Raven.

"So I'll get Billy and I guess the three of us'll go into town and get a little something wet to replace all the sweat we've lost," said the man with a smile.

"I guess so."

"Always assuming Holliday's gotten over his grudge."

"*Doc* Holliday?" asked Raven.

The man smiled. "You know any other Hollidays who go around killing people?"

"None," said Raven nervously. Then: "What's he mad about?"

"This time?" said his companion. "Who the hell knows? You know Doc. It doesn't take much to tick him off."

"So I've heard."

The young man laughed. "So you've *seen*, Ike."

Ike? thought Raven. *I'm Ike, and I'm in Tombstone, and Doc Holliday doesn't like me? Good Lord—I'm Ike Clanton!*

A young man approached them on foot. "Morning, all."

"It's past noon," said Raven's companion.

"I was up most of the night with Chiquita over at the Golden Eagle," said the young man with a grin. "I ain't an old man like my brothers. This is still *my* morning."

Okay, you're Billy Clanton. But who's this other guy?

"Watch yourself, or *this* brother may just turn you over his knee and give you the whipping of your life," said the man.

Ah! You must be Phineas, the other brother. Glad I read up on all you guys when I was a kid.

"Let's ride into town, grab something to drink, and save the whipping for those who deserve it," said Raven.

"You just may be in luck," said Billy. "I saw four of them at the Oriental last night."

"That's a lot," agreed Phin. "But there's a fifth."

"Virgil was out patrolling the streets," answered Billy. "We ran into each other near Fremont Street."

"Did he give you a hard time?"

Billy smiled. "He's an Earp, I'm a Clanton. What do you think?"

"His day is coming," said Phin without returning the smile.

They walked over to the corral, retrieved and saddled their horses, and then began riding. Raven let Phin and Billy show the way, since he had no idea where Tombstone was. They waved to a few farmers who were tending cattle, stopped at a shallow creek to let their mounts get a drink, and then continued, and in another ten minutes Raven could see the dusty, truly unimpressive town in the distance.

"So where are we going?" he asked.

"I like the Golden Eagle," said Billy, "but since Chiquita's probably asleep, it makes no difference to me."

"Nor me," said Phin. "Hell, I'll even go to the Oriental if you're up to it."

Billy made a face. "It's a little early in the day for a shootout."

"Oh, come on," said Phin. "They ain't gonna want their own bar shot up."

"You think Doc Holliday gives a damn?" Billy shot back.

Phin sighed deeply. "You got a point. You know, Johnny Ringo's in the area. Maybe we could kinda sorta arrange a meeting betwixt 'em."

Raven smiled.

"What's so funny, Ike?" demanded Phin.

"Doc and Ringo," answered Raven.

"I repeat, what's so funny?"

"The two fastest guns in the West are also the only two

with college degrees. They're probably as likely to sit down and discuss Shakespeare as shoot each other."

"Cute notion," said Billy. "But I say we hire Ringo to work the herds anyway."

"Ringo doesn't work herds," said Phin.

"To *protect* the herds," amended Billy. "And more to the point, to help protect the herd owners."

"The *current* herd owners," noted Phin with a smile.

"You know, you can be a real pain," said Billy.

"Take it easy," said Raven. "There's enough brothers to be mad at without including our own."

Billy was silent for a moment, then shrugged. "I'm sorry, Phin."

"Me, too, Billy," said Phin. "Let's remember who the bad guys are."

They rode in silence until they entered the town, rode another fifty yards, and stopped at a tavern.

"This is a new one," said Billy. "They were building it last week. I don't think it's even got a name yet."

Raven frowned. "Is it open?"

As the words left his mouth, two cowboys walked out through the swinging doors, strolled over to the nearest hitching post, untied their horses, mounted them, and rode off.

"I guess that answers your question," said Billy with a smile.

"Nice to know we're not the only ones who drink before noon," said Phin.

Raven took a quick look at where his wristwatch had been, found nothing but an empty wrist, then on a hunch checked his vest's pocket, pulled out a watch, and confirmed that it was 11:30 in the morning.

"Okay," said Phin, dismounting. "Let's see what this joint's got."

"Same as all the others, I would imagine," said Raven.

"We also need to see if they've got a faro table, or maybe even a pool table."

"A pool table?" scoffed Phin. "Out here in Tombstone? You've got to be kidding. Or dreaming."

They walked in through the swinging doors.

"*Shit!*" whispered Billy.

"What is it?" asked Raven.

"They don't have any gaming tables," said Billy softly. "But"—he stared at a lone man at a table along the far wall—"they've got a dentist."

Raven didn't have to be told Billy was referring to Doc Holliday. He may or may not have been the only dentist in town, but he was the only one who could elicit that kind of reaction.

Raven stared at the man, who was thin to the point of emaciation. *One hundred twenty pounds,* thought Raven. *One thirty, max. And he's close to six feet tall. Yeah, he's tubercular, all right.*

Holliday wore a thick mustache, was dressed in a black frock coat and black pants, and Raven could see that he had a knife suspended on a very thin string around his neck—so thin that even someone as weak as he appeared to be could pull and break the string with almost no effort. He had a pistol in a holster, and for all Raven knew he had another one in his coat. Appearances, he knew, could be deceiving, but it looked like it had been a long time since Holliday had smiled.

The three Clantons walked up to the bar. Billy and Phin

ordered whiskey, and Raven asked for a beer. After they'd been served, they choose the table that was farthest from Holliday.

"Been meaning to have a little chat with you," said Holliday in a thick Southern accent, never raising his voice.

They stared at him without answering.

"Wyatt was wondering when you plan to return the horse you stole from him," continued Holliday. "I told him that if I saw you before he did, I'd ask."

"We're not horse thieves," said Billy.

You lie well, brother, thought Raven. *I think I'll let you do most of the talking for us. I could never say that with a straight face.*

"Yeah, I know, you're pure as the driven snow," said Holliday, "not that I expect any of you bumpkins to know what snow is. But Wyatt was especially fond of that horse, and he wants it back. Or have you already sold it to the Mexicans?"

"I told you . . ." began Billy.

"I know what you told me," said Holliday, never raising his voice. "Now let me tell you something."

"What?"

"I don't like being lied to."

"What do you think you're gonna do about it?" said Billy belligerently.

"Shut up, Billy!" whispered Raven.

"Funny you should ask," said Holliday, turning on his chair to face them.

"We don't have the horse," said Raven. "But I give you my word that if it turns up, we'll let you and Wyatt know right away and bring it to him."

Holliday stared at him coldly for a long moment. "I hope you mean it," he said at last, turning back to his drink.

"Damn it, Ike!" snapped Billy. "You made it look like I was backing down."

"Trust me," said Raven. "You don't want to go one-on-one with Doc Holliday. With one of the Earps, perhaps—but not him."

"He's drunk as a skunk!" growled Billy. "I could have taken him."

"He was just as drunk the last ten or twenty or fifty men he killed," said Raven. "He probably hasn't drawn a sober breath since he came West after the Civil War."

"That's curious," said Phin.

"What is?" asked Raven.

"Everyone I know, including you, just calls it the war. Or, once in a long while, the War Between the States. I ain't never heard it called the Civil War before."

Shit! thought Raven. *I've got to be more careful.* "I just saw it called that in some magazine."

"Since when you do you read magazines?"

Great! It took me ten whole seconds to screw up again. "In some shop in town," said Raven. "I don't remember which."

"Well," said Billy, "as long as we're in town, I think I'll visit one of the floozies over at Dora's."

"Diddlin' Dora's," said Phin with a smile. "She sure calls a spade a spade."

"Five years from now no one will remember it," said Billy, getting to his feet. "Hell, the mines are almost played out already. Twenty years from now no one will even know a town called Tombstone ever existed."

If you only knew, thought Raven as Billy walked out into the street.

Phin poured them each another drink. They downed it and sat in silence for a few minutes. Then Holliday got up and began walking toward the door, but first he stopped at their table.

"If you want that young man to ever celebrate another birthday, you'd better teach him some manners," he said.

"He's just a kid," said Raven.

"If he lives a few more years he'll be a Clanton man," said Holliday. "And that's not necessarily an improvement."

Raven was still searching his brain for a non-aggressive, non-obsequious reply when Holliday walked out of the saloon and began heading down the wooden sidewalk.

"Sooner or later we're going to have to face him and all those damned Earps," said Phin.

Raven was about to deny it when he realized that of course such a showdown would happen, and it would be exactly the thing that stopped Tombstone from being another forgotten mining town.

"I know," said Raven with a sigh. "But at least we'll pick the time and place."

"And the conditions," added Phin. "Never forget the conditions." Suddenly he chuckled. "Hell, if we could keep Doc off the booze for forty-eight hours I bet he couldn't even see you from twenty feet away, let alone put a bullet into you."

"Great," said Raven. "That would leave only five Earps for us to face."

"Three," replied Phin. "James and Warren aren't around much."

"That makes everything okay," said Raven. "We'd just have to face the three deadliest of the clan."

"Three of us, three of them," said Phin. "What could be fairer?"

This is Wyatt Earp and his brothers you're talking about, thought Raven. *I admire your notion of a fair fight.*

"Well, where are we going now?" asked Phin.

Raven shrugged. "I don't know. I just felt it was too early to keep drinking, and the farther we get from Holliday the better I'll like it."

"Well, there's a place a block to the left that makes pretty good eggs, and the sausage is at least edible. You interested?"

"Not really."

"I didn't think so," said Phin. "Well, I could do with a little food. I'll run into you later, or see you back at the ranch. Don't forget we've got a herd coming in from across the border."

"I won't forget," said Raven.

Phin walked a few steps to the corner, then turned to his left, and Raven decided to spend a little time exploring Tombstone as he was stuck here until (he assumed) he killed the enemy or they killed him.

He passed a leather goods shop, an impressive store that sold everything from saddles to buggy whips to holsters, then came to a barber shop that seemed to specialize not in haircuts but in shaves.

He looked in through the window for a minute, then turned back and headed down the sidewalk—and stopped dead in his tracks.

"Lisa?" he said, half certain, half curious.

She turned to face him, and held a finger to her lips. "Call me Kate," she said in her familiar voice.

"I was afraid I wasn't going to see you on this . . . *excursion*," said Raven. "I can't tell you how relieved I am."

"I was just coming to meet you," she said. "I got word that you were at that just-opened tavern." Suddenly she frowned. "You should be more careful. Doc was on his way there this morning."

"How did you know that?"

"He told me."

"You know him?" asked Raven.

Suddenly her features changed. She added abut thirty pounds, her hair was done up in a bun, her cheeks were fuller, her lips thicker, and her nose larger.

"Omygod!" exclaimed Raven. "You're Big Nose Kate!"

"For the time being."

"Doc's lover," he said disapprovingly.

"He's too drunk and too sick to perform that particular function," she replied. "But I share his room with him, and that way I find out what his plans are."

"He hasn't harmed you?" persisted Raven.

"Eddie, he hasn't so much as touched me."

"You couldn't have been some other woman in Tombstone?"

"None that would be privy to information that might prove useful to you—who's coming for you, where they plan to meet you, and when."

"Okay," he said, trying to relax. "I don't have a calendar, and even if I did I don't know what day the Gunfight at the O.K. Corral takes place. Can you enlighten me?"

"When I have to," said Lisa. "But for the time being, our job is to *avoid* a shoot-out between the two sides." She looked over his shoulder. "We'll talk at dinnertime. Have someone tell you where the Fatted Calf is. Be there at five in the afternoon."

"Why can't we talk now?" he asked, frowning.

"Because Doc is headed this way, and I don't want him to think we've been flirting."

"We haven't been."

"You know and I know it, but Doc will never believe it. Please go!"

He began walking away, and paused just long enough to see her waving a handkerchief at Doc and calling him over to her.

Then he turned a corner, and was half surprised that Holliday wasn't right on his tail.

20

Raven rode back to the ranch alone, his mind working furiously.

Sooner or later there have to be some confrontations, hopefully long before the O.K. Corral. I feel like Eddie Raven, but in this world I'm Ike Clanton, with a reputation for being a mean, tough outlaw. So theoretically no one should be able to push me around, and from what little I've read about this era, Ike wasn't afraid of Doc or the Earps.

Just a minute! I'm remembering more. The Clantons weren't a gang of three—or four, including Old Man Clanton, who I haven't even seen yet. They had a staff of full-time cattle and horse herders—well, cattle and horse thieves, actually— and part-time gunslingers, who were known as the Cowboys. And they had allies. I know about Johnny Ringo, but there was also Curly Bill Brocius, a hell of a formidable man himself. And there's Sheriff Johnny Behan, who had his own reasons for hating the Earps and the publicity they accrued as lawmen, and should be on our side if it comes down to a confrontation.

The more he remembered, the better he felt. When he began riding back to the ranch, he felt overwhelmed, as if the entire territory was opposed to the Clantons—but now that he had begun remembering his history, he realized that the Clantons had far more allies than the Earps.

"Which makes sense," he muttered. "Who the hell supports an ill-tempered, hard-drinking sheriff and his even worse-tempered brothers? It's the Earps and Holliday against the whole damned county, and now that I know what's coming, maybe I can survive it and put history right."

Or at least get home in one piece, he added mentally.

He reached the ranch in another forty minutes, just in time to have his way blocked by sixty or seventy unbranded horses.

"Hi, Ike!" called an old man who was mounted on one of the only branded horses in the bunch. "Give us a hand with this batch!"

Doing what?

"Ride along the left, stop any of 'em from bolting toward town," said the old man as if reading Raven's mind. He turned to the four men who were accompanying him. "Herd 'em into the north pasture."

Raven moved his horse into position, hoping none of the unbranded horses tried to bolt past him, since he had no idea how to stop them.

"Are my two other sons around, or out getting drunk and wearing out the local ladies of the night?"

"Probably a little of each," answered Raven.

"Well, what the hell," said Old Man Clanton. "At least I raised 'em with a proper set of values." Suddenly he turned to one of the men. "Not *that* one!" he yelled. "That chestnut gelding! Take him into the barn and put him in a stall."

"You gonna keep him for yourself?" asked Raven, who

couldn't care less but felt it was a polite question to ask of his father.

"Not for long," replied Old Man Clanton. "That's Wyatt's horse. I covered the brand with some mud, but it'll flake off in a day or two. Eventually we'll sell it back to him, but I know that bastard. Once he hears that we brought in another herd to sell—and he'll know it before nightfall—he'll have his spies sneaking out here to steal his horse back."

Raven wanted to ask why they didn't just *give* it back and avoid any hassle, but realized that such an action was unthinkable to his family.

They had all the horses corralled in another half hour, and then Raven and Old Man Clanton went into the farmhouse.

"Rough trip," commented the old man. "I'll swear they've hired a dozen *federales* and posted them at the border just to stop an old man who never did them any harm from making a living."

"Well, we *do* steal horses and cattle from Mexico," replied Raven.

"Not from the goddamned border police!" snapped Old Man Clanton. "We've never robbed *them*, never even taken a shot at them despite all the justification they've given us."

"Sorry," said Raven, trying not to smile. "I lost my head."

Old Man Clanton stared at him. "I would never tell you not to drink, but you been drinkin' the wrong stuff." He lit up a small, bent cigar. "When are Billy and Phin due back?"

Raven shrugged. "They didn't say."

"Well, we'll assume it'll be in time for dinner." Suddenly the old man grinned. "And if not, that's the only food they're gonna get tomorrow and the day after, until it's gone."

I'm starting to understand why the Clantons are such bastards, thought Raven wryly.

"Well, I ain't et since sunrise," said Old Man Clanton. "I'm off to the kitchen to see what we've got lying around."

"Same as always, I'd suppose," said Raven.

"That's what I mean," said the old man, getting up and walking off to what Raven assumed was the kitchen.

Raven spent the next hour walking around the house, the barn, and the fenced pastures, trying to get a feel for his temporary home. As he was just finishing his tour he saw a rider approaching, and as the horse got closer he could see that it was Phin—but not the way he'd last see him. His face was blood-streaked, his left ear was all but shredded, and his nose was clearly broken.

Raven ran up to him and helped him dismount, where he stood unsteadily on his feet.

"What the hell happened?" asked Raven.

"I was in the Crystal Palace, having a drink with some friends . . ."

"Your *friends* did this?"

Phin forced his battered face into a frown. "Don't be an ass," he said. "We got to talking about women, and the subject got around to sportin' houses, and I mentioned a night I'd spent with Big Nose Kate Elder at the house she ran back in Dodge." He paused and tried to wince. "I hadn't noticed that Doc was standing at the bar, but the next second he was pistol-whipping me and warning me never to mention her name again."

"And none of your friends stood up for you?"

"Against *Doc Holliday*?"

"Stupid question," apologized Raven. "Okay, let's get you

cleaned and patched up." Raven suddenly realized that he didn't know where any of the supplies were, or even if there was any running water in the house. "Lead the way."

"I'll take care of it myself," muttered Phin, starting to walk away.

"Dad's sleeping, so try not to groan or yelp too much."

"I'm a Clanton," replied Phin with all the dignity he could muster, which at the moment wasn't much.

Not necessarily a guarantee of longevity, thought Raven grimly.

He sat back down, lost in thought, until Phin returned perhaps half an hour later.

"Well, the bleeding's stopped," remarked Raven, staring at him. "If you ever want your nose to be straight and true again, we'll have to rebreak it somewhere up the road."

"It's been a rough day," said Phin. "I'm gonna go take a nap. Wake me for dinner."

"I will," said Raven as Phin limped out of the room.

Raven, who had considered himself a bit of a drinker before his Tombstone incarnation, heated up a pot of coffee, poured himself a cup, carried it out to the farmhouse's front porch, and sat down on a rocking chair.

He wasn't really a fan of this kind of hot, cloudless, dusty landscape, but he had to admit it was growing on him. Everything was so still, it had probably looked exactly the same before the house was built.

Except for the cloud of dust approaching him.

He stared at it, and after a couple of minutes was able to make out a horse and rider, though they were still too far away from him to make out any details on either of them. He wondered if he should alert anyone, but Phin was still pretty messed up and the old man wasn't likely to be much help if indeed he found that he needed help.

So he sat, and drank his coffee, and watched as the rider approached. Finally he saw that he was a tall, well-built man with the thick mustache that seemed to be de rigueur out here. He thought the man looked vaguely familiar, not that he'd met him in this incarnation, but rather that he'd seen photos of him.

The man rode his horse right up to the house, pulled him to a stop, and dismounted. There was a hitching post off to the side of the porch, and the man tied his mount's reins to it.

"Howdy, Ike," he said, and it was clear that they knew each other.

"Hi," said Raven, trying to remember who the face belonged to.

"Got word that you were expecting a little trouble with the Earps and the book-reading lunger," said the man.

"It's possible," answered Raven.

"Then it's a damned good thing for you that I was in the area—always assuming that you've got my fee." Suddenly he grinned. "As you know, John Ringo don't come cheap."

Ringo! Of course!

"No one ever suggested John Ringo isn't worth what he charges," said Raven.

Ringo laughed. "Damn! They always said you were the brightest of the Clantons!" He paused. "Got a room in the house?"

"No, but you can board with the Cowboys."

Ringo made a face. "I think I'll get a room in town. I've been told that the Grand Hotel's pretty nice." Suddenly he smiled.

"They tell me that's where Big Nose Kate does most of her drinking. Having me on the premises will drive the Doc absolutely crazy." He paused. "Besides, unless I miss my guess, he's one of the guys you'd like to be rid of."

"It wouldn't make me unhappy," said Raven.

Ringo laughed again. "Sounds like we're in business."

Except that you never shot it out with Doc Holliday. No one knows how the hell you were killed, but Doc died in a sanitarium six or seven years from now. Still, why discourage you? If it'll take Doc's concentration off the Clantons for the length of time you're here, so much the better.

"So who's the rest of the opposition?"

"The Earps," answered Raven.

"Wyatt and Virgil for sure," said Ringo, nodding his head. "What about the other three?"

"I haven't seen James or Warren since I got to town," said Raven. "From a cattle drive," he added quickly. "Morgan's here; I think he's one of Virgil's deputies."

"So there are only three of them," said Ringo. "And in terms of skill, one of 'em's pretty useless." He paused. "I understand there's even a sixth brother somewhere. You'd think Old Man Earp could have found a more useful way to spend his spare time."

"So you're definitely with us?" persisted Raven.

"Long as you pay my fee."

"Done."

Ringo reached out his hand, and Raven took and shook it.

My God, I've just hired a notorious killer to shoot another notorious killer, and a trio of notorious lawmen. This is not something the Garment District exactly prepared me for.

"You want me to call them out when I get to town?" asked Ringo.

And face four-to-one odds? Good as you are, I can't believe you're that good.

"No, we'll set something up and tip you off when it's just about ready."

"No problem, as long as they stay out of the Grand Hotel," said Ringo. He walked over to his horse, untied the reins, and mounted it. "See you soon, Ike."

"Right," said Raven. "And thanks, John."

"Make it Johnny," said Ringo with a smile. "I'm being friendlier these days."

He wheeled his horse around and headed off toward Tombstone.

Well, that solves that. Doc's going to be so busy with Ringo that he's not going to have any time for the Clantons.

Then it struck him.

Good God! Lisa will be with Doc. She could wind up in the line of fire! I'd better get to town and warn her that it's time to go on a trip, anywhere that Doc isn't.

He waited until he could no longer see the dust Ringo's hose was raising, then saddled up his own horse, put its bridle on, and mounted it. He wished he knew an alternate route to Tombstone, but he'd only been there once, in Billy's and Phin's company, and he wasn't going to take a chance of choosing the wrong direction and giving Ringo most of the day to find Doc if Lisa was with him.

It took him an hour to reach Tombstone, and five minutes later he'd hitched his mount at the Fatted Calf. He checked his wrist, realized he didn't have a watch, estimated that it was midafternoon, and that he had about two hours to kill before Lisa showed up.

"What'll it be, Ike?" called the bartender from behind the polished bar.

"A glass of very cold water," said Raven.

"Come on, no kidding now."

"Okay, a beer."

"Ain't got none. You know that."

"Okay," said Raven. "You choose."

The bartender nodded. "The usual."

He poured a glass of whiskey and set it on the bar, and Raven realized that he was expected to walk over and pick it up, which he did, returning with it to his table. Two or three customers gave him friendly greetings, which he returned, but thankfully no one seemed interested in starting a conversation with him, which meant he wouldn't make any verbal blunders.

He managed to nurse the drink for almost an hour. Then he saw Big Nose Kate Elder's face peek in over the swinging doors. She smiled and walked over to join him at his table.

"How's it going, Eddie?" she asked.

"I'm not sure. But I know we've got to talk."

"That's why I'm here."

He stared at her and took a deep breath. "You've got to get out of Tombstone right away."

She frowned. "What is this about."

"John Ringo paid us a visit at the ranch. He'd heard that Doc and the Earps had a grudge against the Clantons, and offered to help us."

"Interesting."

He shook his head vigorously. "It's more than interesting,

Lisa! It could be deadly. The one he wants most seems to be Doc. If they get into a shoot-out, you don't want to be a nearby bystander."

"It's all right, Eddie," she said with a smile.

"Damn it, Kate!" he snapped. "They're the two most deadly killers in the Old West!"

"Yes, I know."

"Then you can't be anywhere near them when they meet."

She reached her hand across the table. "Hold my hand, Eddie."

He frowned, but did as she asked.

With her free hand she pulled a small dagger out of her purse and handed it to him.

"What do you think of this?" she asked.

"It's a knife," said Raven.

"A real one?" she persisted. "Not phony in any way?"

He examined it more carefully, even pricked his thumb with it and drew blood.

"Yes, it's real, all right."

"You're sure?"

"Yes, I'm sure," he said, wondering where this was leading.

"Good," she said, reaching her hand out and turning it palm up. "Now stab me."

He frowned. "What the hell are you talking about."

"Just do it, Eddie."

"Hell, no!"

"I insist, Eddie!" she said firmly.

He touched her palm gently with the point of the knife.

"Now push down!" she snapped.

He didn't know why, maybe it was the authority in her

voice, or the fear of so upsetting her with his disobedience that he'd lose her, but he took a deep breath and plunged the knife down.

It went completely through her hand, encountering no resistance, and buried itself in the table.

She smiled and pulled back her unmarked hand.

"I don't understand," said Raven, frowning.

"I am the Mistress of Illusions," she said. "Neither your knife nor anyone's bullets are going to harm me."

He simply stared at her as the truth of her words sank in.

"I dislike that little demonstration, Eddie," she continued, "but I had to prove to you that I'm in no danger even if Doc and Ringo start shooting at each other and I'm standing between them."

"Give me a few minutes to get over the shock and I'll tell you how relieved I am," said Raven.

She smiled. It was Kate Elder's smile, but somehow Lisa's face peeked through, if only to Raven and if only for a second or two.

"So what plans have you made, besides hiring one shooter to face another?"

"Nothing yet," he said. "Hell, I haven't even met the Earps yet."

"Don't wait too long," she said.

"I know, I know," replied Raven.

"I hope so," she said. "This is not a town that any sane man wants to live or die in."

21

R aven sat alone in the bar for ten minutes after Lisa left, considering what she had told him and trying to dope out his plan of action.

Finally he got to his feet and walked to the door. He was about to go out onto the sidewalk when John Ringo entered the saloon.

"Hi, Ike," he said. "I thought you'd be hiding back at the ranch."

"Why hide now that you're on our side?" shot back Raven.

Ringo chuckled and slapped him on the shoulder. "Damn! I knew I liked you!"

"So have you got your bearings yet?" asked Raven.

"I found my hotel, I've located the half-dozen best bars in town and paid my respects to five of them."

"Just five?" asked Raven with a smile.

"I thought I'd give the Oriental a pass," said Ringo. "Too damned many Earps."

"Makes sense," acknowledged Raven.

"Oh, I'll kill 'em all sooner or later, but there ain't no sense taking on four or five of 'em at once if I don't have to." He smiled. "Besides, I keep hoping I'll run into Holliday first. I saw his woman leave here a few minutes ago, and half hoped I'd find him here." He shook his head. "For a woman as famous as Big Nose Kate is, she sure ain't much to look at."

"She has hidden qualities."

"Oh?" said Ringo. "Such as?"

Raven smiled. "Hidden."

"On my way to town from your ranch, I ran into Curly Bill Brocius. He was heading out to have a powwow with your old man. Anything come of it?"

"He'll be working with us," answered Raven. "I think he hates Doc and the Earps almost as much as you do."

"I don't hate anyone," replied Ringo. "I just like the biggest challenge, and they offer it." He chuckled. "Hell, I've seen Holliday once in my life, and that's once more than any of the Earps."

Raven stared at him. "You mean it, don't you?"

"Right."

"And it's just the challenge?" continued Raven. "It's nothing personal?"

"When you're the best, you have to keep proving it." He snorted contemptuously. "Hell, most of Tombstone thinks Doc is the best. I got a reputation to defend."

"Well, the Clantons will do everything we can to help you convince the townsfolk they were wrong." *And I think it had better be soon. I can't remember the date of the Gunfight at the O.K. Corral, but it can't be too far off.*

"Just steer clear when I go up against him."

"Only a crazy man would stand between you two," said Raven sincerely.

The problem is that history says you're not at the O.K. Cor-

ral, and Doc lives another five or six years. And Wyatt Earp lives long enough to advise Tom Mix how to play a cowboy in the movies. Rofocale, Lisa—I hope you're tuning in on my thoughts, because I sure as hell don't see how this is going to work out.

"Well, I'm going to get a little something to drink," said Ringo, heading toward the bar. "Care to join me? Your treat, of course."

"No, I've had my share for the daylight. Maybe I'll come by later—to this joint or another."

Raven walked out the door, looked up and down the street, didn't see Lisa in her Kate identity or as herself, and began wandering through the streets, trying to get the feel of the place. He came to a stop when he saw the Oriental a block away, checked the street signs and fixed its location in his memory, then turned back the way he had come.

He passed a butcher shop without even looking in the window—if there was one thing the Clanton ranch wasn't lacking, it was meat—and before long came to where he'd hitched his horse. He noticed that the water trough next to the post had gone dry, so he walked his horse to a half-full one a few yards away, waited for him to take a drink, then mounted him and began riding back to the ranch.

Damn it! he thought. *Is anybody there?*

Yes, Eddie, came Rofocale's thought. *One of us is.*

You know the situation. No matter how I try to alter history, Doc and the Earps all live through the gunfight and there's no record of Ringo being involved in it.

That is true.

Then why the hell am I going through these efforts?

Because if you were truly Ike Clanton, that is precisely what you would do.

Okay, I know, it's a test—but haven't I passed it by at least trying *to get Ringo to insert himself before the gunfight. And maybe getting Brocius and the Cowboys to nullify the Earps.*

Your behavior thus far has been exemplary, replied Rofocale.

Then get me the hell out of here before everything goes wrong and Doc and the Earps kill the Clanton gang.

When the time comes, said Rofocale.

When what *time comes?* demanded Raven.

When you have completed your test.

I don't understand.

I intuit that anything further I say will just confuse you.

I'm confused already, said Raven irritably.

Signing off, said Rofocale, and suddenly his presence was gone from inside Raven's head.

"Great!" muttered Raven. "That was just phase one of this idiot test. I guess phase two is to die with some semblance of dignity, or maybe to ride hell-for-leather until I'm on the other side of the Mississippi."

Don't be foolish, Eddie, said Lisa's voice.

You've been listening? Can you tell me what the hell is going on?

But there was no answer, and her presence, like Rofocale's, had left his consciousness.

"All right," he said. "I'm stuck here. Ringo's on our side. So is Brocius. If we go to the O.K. Corral with both of them, and maybe half a dozen Cowboys, maybe we can win, or at least scare 'em off until they can even up the odds." He paused, considering the situation. "And maybe I can get that sheriff—*our* sheriff—Johnny Behan to tell the Earps that if they precipitate a gunfight the surviving Earps are all going to jail." He turned his horse around and headed back into town. "Maybe I'd better have a talk with this Behan before the Earps do."

When he got back to town, he rode up and down a trio of streets until he came to a frame building with steel bars on all the windows, and a large Sherriff's Office sign hanging down in the front. Raven dismounted, hitched his horse, pretended to fuss with the saddle for a moment until his heart stopped racing, and walked in the front door.

"Howdy, Ike!" enthused the man with the sheriff's badge.

"Hi, Sheriff."

"Screw the 'Sheriff,'" said Behan. "You're Ike, I'm Johnny."

"Sorry, Johnny," said Raven. "Been a hard day."

"The rest of it ought to be a little easier," said Behan. "I see Johnny Ringo's in town."

Raven held up his right hand and crossed his index and middle fingers. "Hopefully he'll do our job for all of us."

"That thought has crossed my mind," said Behan with a chuckle.

"But," continued Raven.

"But?"

"But if it comes to a fight, I assume you'll back us up?"

"Not with a gun, that's for damned sure," said Behan. "But I'll throw any Earp who survives it into jail."

"And Doc?"

"That's a little harder," admitted Behan. "Still, that's what I got deputies for."

"Good. I just wanted to hear you say it."

"You know I got no use for those scum." Behan grimaced. "You know Virgil deputizes the whole damned family, so they think they're responsible to no one except maybe the God of the Earps." A malicious smile crossed his face. "Them what survives are gonna find out how wrong they are."

"Just hold that thought," said Raven.

Behan pulled a bottle out of a desk drawer. "Care for one?"

My God, is every resident of this town an alcoholic?

"No, thanks, Johnny. I've got to be getting back to the ranch. Dad was pretty used up when he got in. I want to make sure he's okay."

"Okay," said Behan. "And keep an eye out for Wyatt or one of the other scum. He seems to think you've got his horse there."

"Thanks for the warning."

"You don't, do you?" asked Behan.

"Not to my knowledge," lied Raven, which he decided would be his position and his excuse if anyone spotted the horse.

"Well, give Billy and Phin my best."

"Will do," said Raven, walking to the door, opening it, and going back into the street, where he unhitched his horse, mounted it, and hoped he could make it home without encountering another offer of a drink.

22

Upon arriving back at the ranch Raven was approached by Curly Bill Brocius, a massive man with a head of thick, curly hair, as befit his name.

"Glad you're back, Ike," said Brocius.

"Is something wrong?"

"Not yet," said Brocius. "But we've got Wyatt's horse here. The markings and brand are unmistakable. Sooner or later he's going to come out here after him."

"Later, I hope," said Raven.

Brocius threw back his head and laughed. "I've always liked your sense of humor, Ike."

"Thanks, I guess."

"But it doesn't alter the fact that Wyatt or one of them other goddamned Earps is going to be out here sooner or later, probably sooner, looking for his horse." He paused briefly. "There's a farm about thirty miles east of here that'll take it for a few months."

"Out of the goodness of their hearts?" asked Raven.

"That, plus a hundred dollars."

Raven shook his head. "Just to watch a horse that no one's going to ride out that far to look at?"

"Up to you," said Brocius. Suddenly he grinned. "No way it's gonna cost us a hundred dollars in bullets."

"Ah!" replied Raven with a smile. "An optimist."

Brocius smiled again, and shook his head. "Out here we're all pessimists. The optimists are the ones who think they'll see another sunrise or two."

"There's a lot of us and not that many of them," said Raven.

"Yeah, that makes a difference. It's not like going up against Ringo or the Doc, where one of them figures to beat eight or ten guys at once."

"You really think they're that good?" asked Raven curiously.

"I really think I wouldn't care to find out," said Brocius devoutly.

"Everyone makes it sound like there's two superbeings with guns—Doc and Ringo—and no one else has a chance," remarked Raven.

"Well, in Tombstone," answered Brocius. "They say John Wesley Hardin could give either of them a hell of a fight, but last anyone heard he's rotting in a jail in Texas."

"And there's always Wild Bill Hickok," said Raven.

Brocius stared at him. "What you been drinking, Ike? Hickok got himself killed four years ago. And besides, except for one lucky shot against a nobody, he was never that good."

"I bow to your expertise."

"Well, I'm off to get a little grub. Want to come along?"

Raven shook his head. "No, I want to check on the old man, and see if Phin or Billy have encountered any problems I should know about."

"You mean any not named Doc or Wyatt," said Brocius with a grin.

"Those too," answered Raven.

Brocius walked off to the bunkhouse, and Raven entered the farmhouse. His father was sitting on a rocking chair, looking a lot better than the last time he'd seen him.

"How're you doing, Dad?"

"I'll be okay," answered the old man. "I'm just not up to a three-day horse-and-cattle drive anymore."

"Nothing to be ashamed of. Next time just send Phin in your place."

"Yeah, makes sense," said Old Man Clanton. "Wyatt come looking for his goddamned horse yet?"

"No, but I think we can be pretty sure that sooner or later he will."

"I saw Curly Bill and his men moving their stuff into the bunkhouse. Good idea."

"Glad you approve."

"Now if you can just get Johnny Ringo . . ."

"We got him."

"Really?" asked the old man excitedly.

"Really," answered Raven. "I don't know for how long."

"What's he costing us?"

"Almost nothing."

Old Man Clanton frowned. "A man like Ringo? That doesn't make any sense."

"I think he just wants the opportunity to prove he can beat Holliday in a gunfight."

"Well, let's hope his confidence is justified."

The front door opened, and Billy Clanton walked in. "Hot out there," he remarked.

"And you're surprised?" said Old Man Clanton in amused tones.

"You know, they've started making book on the coming fight."

"Doc and Ringo?" asked Raven.

"Well, actually, they're making book on *two* fights," answered Billy. "Doc and Ringo, of course. And the Earps and the Clantons."

"I'd ask who's favorite in the second fight, but it might depress me," said Raven.

"They just set it up maybe an hour ago," said Billy. He paused. "Odds were pretty much even when I left."

"On *both* fights?" asked Old Man Clanton.

"On Doc and Ringo."

"What about us and the Earps?"

Billy grimaced. "They're the favorite."

"Close?"

"Heavy," said Billy unhappily.

"Good!" said Old Man Clanton.

"What's so good about being such an underdog?" asked Raven.

"You ain't thinking this through, youngster," said the old man. "We put every last penny we've got on ourselves. Even mortgage the ranch and anything else we own." Suddenly he offered a near-toothless grin. "If we win, we all get rich."

"And if we lose?" said Billy.

The grin remained. "If we lose, we ain't gonna need no money where we're headed."

Billy turned to Raven. "He's got a point."

"Yes, he does," agreed Raven. "But it's a very final point. I'd like to see if we can avoid a gunfight."

"Everyone's been expecting one."

"We're not everyone," said Raven. "We're Clantons, and I see no reason to put our lives on the line to make everyone else happy." *And my memory is that you were the first one killed at O.K. Corral.*

"Well," said Billy, "I suppose one thing we can do is lead Wyatt's horse to the played-out silver mines at the far end of town in the middle of the night, turn him loose, and there's no way Wyatt can prove we had anything to do with it."

Raven turned to the old man. "You think Wyatt would buy that we had nothing to do with it?"

"Not a chance. Hell, a couple of my Mexicans were so anxious to tell him about it they cut out a day early so they could race ahead and let him know."

Raven frowned. "Then why isn't he here already?"

"Probably got business in town or at the Oriental," said Old Man Clanton. "He knows we're not going anywhere, and neither is his damned horse."

"Okay," said Raven. "But we'd better keep a round-the-clock watch for him."

"Why?" said the old man. "He ain't coming out in the dark. No way he could spot his horse—or see who's aiming at him. Just keep an eye out for him starting each day at sunup."

Raven sighed. "Okay, makes sense."

"I raised you to be brighter, Ike. You should'a thunk of that yourself."

Raven had to restrain himself from yelling "I'm a god-damned dress merchant!" and silently nodded his head.

"Okay," said Billy. "Since Phin ain't back, I'll check on the cattle and horses myself."

"And I think I'll grab a nap before dinner," added the old man, getting slowly, carefully to his feet and hobbling off to his room.

Raven was left alone in the house. He considered everything he'd heard, both in town and back here at the ranch, and finally shook his head.

Is anybody there?

I am, Eddie, came Lisa's thought.

I'm trying, thought Raven, *but I'm just not fit for this.*

Do you think you were fit to be Dracula or Don Quixote?

He frowned. *Those were simple and over fast, nothing as complex as this scenario.*

They were easier, agreed Lisa.

None of them were easy . . . but this one goes on and on. And I know the goddamned outcome. Doc and the Earps kill Billy and the McLaury brothers at O.K. Corral, and the only reason they let me live is because I'm unarmed and I plead for my life. I don't remember a lot of the details, but I sure remember the outcome.

He could almost feel her sigh. *Ah, Eddie—you make me feel so old.*

Well, right now I'm busy feeling doomed, he answered. He paused for a moment, trying to order his thoughts and ignore the fact that she was reading them as quickly as he thought them. *Look, I know you didn't send me here to kill me. But just what am I supposed to do as a goddamned horse and cattle* thief? *I suppose I should help somebody, but I haven't met a single person worth helping since I got here—probably including me.*

Eddie, I can't answer your questions, thought Lisa.

You mean you won't.

Can't, won't, it comes to the same thing. Just as your actions are constricted by being Ike Clanton, mine are constricted as the Mistress of Illusions.

Come on, he thought irritably. *You change eras as easily as I do, you've already shown me that nothing can harm you, you can assume any identity you want while I'd stuck in whatever identity you or Rofocale put me in. You can't be as helpless as you say.*

Not helpless, Eddie, she replied. *Powerless.*

What the hell's the difference?

When you figure it out, you'll be well on your way to solving this test.

And then he was totally alone again, and Lisa's telepathic voice vanished in the late afternoon heat.

23

He joined his father and brothers for dinner, spent a fruit-less hour trying to find something—*anything*—to read, sat out on the porch hoping to make contact with Lisa or Ro-focale, decided after two more hours that it wasn't going to happen, and went to bed.

He got up about an hour after sunrise to find that they had company. John Ringo had stopped by to have a drink with Brocius, and grab a little breakfast.

Even you? thought Raven. *How does anyone stay sober long enough to shoot straight?* And then he decided that the only solution was that the whiskey they brewed out here in the West must be thirty-proof or less. At least, given the fact that he was facing an almost certain gunfight in the near future, he hoped so.

He decided that he ought to walk over to the bunkhouse and make sure Ringo hadn't changed his mind about which side he was on. As he neared his destination, he saw the tops of some books sticking out of Ringo's saddle. He stopped by the horse, pulled out the books, and inspected them: Thucy-dides, Plato, Dante, and Walt Whitman.

"That's a hell of a traveling library for a traveling killer," he muttered softly, carefully placing them back.

"I see you're looking at my reading matter," said Ringo's voice, and Raven turned to see him standing perhaps ten feet away.

"I'm impressed," said Raven. "Just out of curiosity, have you ever met Whitman during your travels?"

Ringo shook his head. "Haven't even cracked the book yet. I picked it up in Dodge, after Doc recommended it." He shrugged. "Of course, that's before we were mortal enemies." A pause. "Not that we were ever friends."

"Well, it's a damned impressive collection," said Raven.

Ringo smiled. "Better than all those lies Ned Buntline publishes in his penny dreadfuls. By last count I'd killed sixty-seven men and a couple of dancing girls who pirouetted into my line of fire."

"Why don't you shootists sue him?" asked Raven.

"I think me, Doc, John Wesley, any of us, would rather kill him," answered Ringo.

Of course you would. I've got to remember who I'm talking to.

"I wonder if I could ask a favor of you, John," said Raven.

"Oh?" said Ringo, suddenly suspicious.

Raven nodded his head. "I'd like a short-term loan of one of your books. I'll give it back before you leave town."

Ringo stared at him. "When did any of the Clantons learn to read?"

"I picked up an interest in it," said Raven. "But we don't have anything to read at the house."

"What the hell," said Ringo with a shrug. "Take the Dante.

At least you can find out what'll happen to you if you lose it or forget to return it."

"Thanks," said Raven. "I'll get it on the way back to the house—unless you're planning on leaving for town right away?"

"No, Curly Bill and I were having a good time discussing old battles when I heard you nosing around and came out to see what was going on." He smiled. "You don't know how rare readers are out here."

"I've got a pretty good idea," said Raven, returning his smile. "Okay, go visit with Curly Bill. Maybe I'll catch you on your way out."

Ringo nodded and went back around the bunkhouse to its door, and after Raven had removed *Inferno* from Ringo's saddlebag he walked back to the ranch house, decided he could live without the kind of breakfast he knew they'd be cooking up, and sat down on a rocking chair, opened the book, and began reading.

He hadn't noticed the passage of time, but he was almost thirty pages into it when Phin Clanton galloped up, dismounted, and tied his horse to a rail.

"Is Curly Bill here?" he asked excitedly.

"Yeah," answered Raven, closing the book and putting it on a table. "He's in the bunkhouse, visiting with John Ringo."

"So much the better!"

"What's the problem?"

"I was coming home after refreshing one of Madam Cleopatra's fallen flowers, and I got word that Morgan Earp was coming out here, all on his own, to find Wyatt's horse. I took the longer route, but"—he pointed to his sweat-soaked mount—"I never let him slow down from a gallop. We've probably got five or ten minutes before he shows."

"Okay," said Raven. "Run over to the bunkhouse and let them know."

"Right," answered Phin, racing over to the bunkhouse.

Raven went inside to see if Billy or the old man were up, and sure enough they were eating breakfast.

"Didn't see no sense waiting for you, Ike," said Old Man Clanton. "Hell, if you eat breakfast three times a week, that's a lot these days."

"Got more important things to discuss than breakfast," said Raven. "Morgan Earp will be here in a couple of minutes, looking for Wyatt's horse." Before Billy or the old man could say anything, Raven held up a hand. "John Ringo's already here, and he and Curly Bill are ready for him."

"Billy," said Old Man Clanton, getting to his feet and hobbling toward the door, "get me my shotgun."

"I'll get us both our shotguns," said Billy, walking off in the other direction.

Raven went outside and posted himself in front of the house. He didn't know what he was going to do, or would be expected to do. He was unarmed, and he figured he couldn't hit the broad side of the bunkhouse from fifty feet away if he *was* carrying a gun. He also knew that a man on foot didn't have much chance of stopping, or even slowing down, a man on horseback.

But he was here, and he felt he had to do *something*.

He saw Ringo and Brocius leave the bunkhouse, followed by Phin, and tried to analyze their attitudes. Phin looked nervous, Brocius anxious, Ringo close to being bored. Which co-incided with Raven's opinion of their abilities.

Ringo saw Raven and nodded to him. Brocius never looked anywhere but the direction of Tombstone. And Phin's head was constantly in motion as he looked behind every tree, bush, horse, and anything else that could temporarily hide a man from view, as well as a hundred things that couldn't.

And just as Raven was concluding that it was a false alarm, that someone had lied to Phin, there was a small cloud of dust on the horizon, and a moment later a lone rider came into view.

Brocius and Phin visibly tensed. Ringo merely drew his pistol a couple times to make sure nothing was slowing or obstructing it, then folded his arms across his chest and waited for the rider to reach the immediate area.

Damn! Is that Morgan Earp? I saw his photo in a history book, but that was in another world, either eons ago or eons from now.

The rider's horse veered and walked directly toward Raven.

"Mornin', Ike," said the rider.

"Mornin', Morgan," answered Raven, and added mentally, *if you* are *Morgan.*

"Got word from one of the men who helped you Clantons steal your latest herd of horses and cattle that Wyatt's horse was in with them. Same description, same brand." Earp smiled a humorless smile. "Now, I know it's probably all a mistake or a misunderstanding, so if you'll just turn him over to me I'll take him back to town and there won't be no trouble."

"We haven't got Wyatt's horse," said Old Man Clanton from the porch, shotgun trained on Earp.

"If you don't mind, I think I'll just have a look around for myself," said Earp, dismounting.

"But we *do* mind," said Ringo, stepping forward and blocking his way.

"So you're the Clantons' hired gun now?"

"No one pays me," said Ringo. "Now mount up and ride home and tell your brothers that they sent you on a wild goose chase."

"And if I don't?" said Earp pugnaciously.

"Then I hope there's a good doctor in town," said Ringo, drawing his gun and cracking it across Earp's face so quickly that his target didn't have time to duck or raise a hand to protect himself.

Earp staggered blindly to his left, blood pouring from a gash on his cheek, and Ringo cracked him on the forehead with the gun, then did it again as Earp dropped to his knees.

Raven had heard or read the term "pistol-whip" sometime in the past, but he'd had no idea how frightening and blood-soaked the act could actually be.

Ringo cracked him across the face a few more times, checked to make sure the now-unconscious man was still breathing, picked him up, and laid him across the top of his horse.

"Bill," he said, turning to Brocius, "lead the horse to within sight of Tombstone, then crack him on the hindquarters and get out of sight before anyone pulls Earp off of him."

"Right," said Brocius, getting his own horse, mounting it, grabbing the reins of Earp's horse, and starting the trip back to town.

Ringo turned to Old Man Clanton. "That's one Earp that ain't gonna bother you in the near future."

"You realize that's gonna bring the other four out here looking for blood," said the old man.

"You're going to face 'em sooner or later," replied Ringo. "Might as well do it on our property, with our men backing us up."

"So you're sticking around?"

Ringo grinned. "I wouldn't miss it for the world."

Old Man Clanton looked at the crew who had been watching from the bunkhouse.

"What the hell are you staring at?" he demanded. "This is a working ranch, so get to work!"

"Give 'em a break," said Phin, emerging from the house. "Hell, he just took Morgan apart maybe two minutes ago."

"*You* pay 'em and they can stand there 'til midnight," said the old man. "If *I'm* footing the bills, they *work*."

"All right," muttered Phin, walking off to the bunkhouse. "I'll tell them."

"Don't worry, old man," said Ringo. "Once you die and he inherits, he won't spend a penny he doesn't have to spend."

"And Ike's next in line anyway," added Old Man Clanton.

Phin glared at him just long enough that Raven found himself wishing the old man had kept his mouth shut.

I hope you were watching, Lisa. Unless every book about the Earps overlooked the pistol-whipping, we just managed to change history in a small way.

Don't celebrate too soon, Eddie, came her voiceless reply. *Because of that, you're going to have the opportunity to change it in a large way.*

What do you mean? asked Raven.

But there was no reply.

Raven busied himself with some trivial duties around the house, and after a couple of hours joined his father and brothers for lunch.

He spent a couple of hours reading the *Inferno* on the porch, and then, at midafternoon, he heard some yells and commotion coming from the bunkhouse. Frowning, he got to his feet and looked across at it—and saw four or five of the men all pointing toward a dust cloud on the horizon.

Ringo walked across to the farmhouse, where the old man, Phin, and Billy had all joined Raven on the porch.

"Better get ready," he said.

"Wyatt?" asked Billy.

"All of 'em," said Ringo. Suddenly he smiled. "Well, all of 'em except Morgan, anyway."

And suddenly Raven could make out the faces and figures of the four grim horsemen.

I didn't want this. They're all going to kill each other.

There was no response from Lisa or Rofocale.

He looked at Wyatt Earp's face. The jaw was set, the eyes unblinking. If there was any hesitation, it would be on one of his brothers' faces . . . but they all wore the same expression.

Then he looked at Ringo, standing along in front of the four riders. Brocius was nearby, so were half-a-dozen ranch hands, but basically it was Ringo standing his ground, staring at the four of them.

Damn it, Rofocale! These aren't Munchkins and I'm not Don Quixote or Dracula! These men really lived!

"I want my horse," said Wyatt Earp.

"Don't look at me," said Ringo. "I'm just a friend of the family."

Earp turned, not to Old Man Clanton, but to Raven. "Okay, Ike," he said. "Hand it over."

Hell, I don't even know what it looks like. "We haven't got it."

"I assume you don't mind if I search through your stock," said Earp.

"And grab the first ten horses you see and claim they're all yours?" replied Raven coldly.

Good God—did I say that?

"I think it'd be best if you ride on," said Ringo. "You need a horse, borrow Morgan's. He ain't going to need it for a while."

"That's something else we have to talk about."

Ringo shook his head. "Nope. I'm all through listening."

Suddenly Virgil, the Earp who was wearing the marshal's badge, went for his gun.

Ringo was quicker, and put a bullet right between his eyes.

Instantly everyone on each side had a gun in his hand. Brocius took a bullet in his arm, fell to his knees, but kept firing. James and Warren Earp both fell out of their saddles; Warren was clearly dead, but James was still firing his weapon.

Ringo turned to face him and prepared to finish him off, and Raven saw that as he did so Wyatt had his gun trained on Ringo.

"*Shit!*" he muttered, finally drawing his own gun, and firing five quick shots in Wyatt's direction. He'd never fired one before, it felt like an alien act to him, but Wyatt fell to the ground and lay motionless.

"Thanks, Ike," said Ringo, walking around and nudging each of the dead Earps with the toe of his boot. When there was no response, he finally holstered his gun.

"They're all dead?" asked Raven. "You're sure?"

"*I'm* sure," said Ringo. "But you can put another bullet into each of them if you've got any doubts."

"I'll take your word for it."

"Well, that's four fewer bastards roaming the West," said Ringo. "I wonder if Morgan will ever figure out just how lucky he was to have come out all by himself yesterday."

If he ever walks and talks again, thought Raven.

"Well, there's nothing more to do here. I'll stick around awhile if you or the old man want, but what the hell, I feel an urge to go into town and celebrate."

"I'll come along later," said Brocius, as he tended his wound. "But we got to clean the place up first." He grinned. "Who knows what kind of critters they'll attract when they start to ripen."

"A telling point," said Raven. "Bill, if you and the crew will load the Earps onto a wagon, I'll go into town with Ringo and dump 'em off at an undertaker's." He turned to Ringo. "Will you wait for me? Shouldn't take ten minutes."

"Of course I will," said Ringo. Suddenly he smiled. "I wouldn't want to be a lone Clanton delivering four dead Earps to the undertaker in Tombstone."

Damn! I hadn't thought of that. Ah, well, there's no way we can keep it a secret, not with so many eyewitnesses and participants.

A few minutes later the bodies were loaded onto the wagon, Raven insisted their horses be hitched to the back of it, and then he and Ringo began what turned out to be his last ride into Tombstone.

24

"Let's unload 'em here," said Ringo as they came to a run-down shed on the edge of town.

"Any particular reason why?" asked Raven.

"He's a sometime undertaker, and like a lot of folks in town, he hates the Earps." Suddenly he smiled. "Perhaps I should say he *hated* the Earps." Ringo dismounted. "You stay there, Ike. This'll just take a minute."

Ringo vanished into the shed, and came out a moment later accompanied by an emaciated man who looked like a grinning ghoul. They shook hands, Ringo unhitched his horse from the wagon, and a moment later he and Raven were riding into Tombstone.

"Word's going to get out pretty soon," noted Raven.

"Hell, half the town'll be celebrating."

"I was thinking of the other half," answered Raven. "Especially one particular member of it."

"He'll be sleeping off last night's drunk for another few hours," answered Ringo. Suddenly he smiled. "Which reminds me, maybe we should get started on ours."

"What the hell," said Raven with a shrug. "It's too early for me to drink, but I'm safer in your company than without it, especially today."

"Haven't been to the Deuces Wild in a week," said Ringo. "That suit you?"

"Anything that gets me out of the public eye suits me."

Ringo laughed. "I don't know how you got a reputation for being such a tough bastard."

"Probably by not going up against you or Wyatt Earp," answered Raven.

Ringo chuckled again, then pulled his horse to a stop.

"What's the matter?" asked Raven.

"They don't allow horses in saloons," answered Ringo. "And we're here."

They dismounted, tied their mounts to the hitching post in front, and entered the Deuces Wild.

"Go get what you want," said Raven. "I'll be sitting at that table by the far wall."

"I can bring you a drink," said Ringo. "Hell, it'll be my treat."

"No, thanks. I'll take coffee if they have it."

Ringo laughed aloud at that. "Some rough tough cowboy!"

Raven walked over to a table while Ringo approached the bar.

Lisa? Can you read me?

Yes, Eddie. I'm on my way over right now. Deuces Wild, correct?

Yes. He paused. *There's been some serious bloodshed.*

I know. I saw it.

You were there?

No, of course not.

I killed Wyatt Earp. Me, not Ringo or Curly Bill. I still don't know quite how it happened.

It'll all come back to you as you calm down.

You're not mad?

Of course not. The alternative would have been for Ringo to bring five *bodies back to town.*

Damn, I miss you!

Count to thirty.

Why?

I'll be there while you're still in the twenties.

Raven suddenly sat up, totally alert, and wished he'd chosen a table next to a window so he could have a view of the street. Then, a few seconds later, a pudgy, once-attractive woman entered the saloon and began approaching him. He was about to suggest she had the wrong bar or at least the wrong person, and then realized it was Lisa in her Kate Elder persona.

"I was wondering if I was ever going to see you again," said Raven.

"I'm not a deserter," she said, sounding somewhat annoyed.

He shook his head. "No, I meant that when the shooting started, given my skills with a gun, I figured the odds were heavy that I wouldn't make it to the end of the fight."

She smiled, reached forward, and laid her hand on his. "You must never underestimate yourself, Eddie," she said. "Neither Rofocale nor I ever have."

"So what's next?" he asked.

She shrugged. "It depends on circumstances."

"*What* circumstances."

She smiled again. "You'll figure it out."

"Okay," he said. "I came to Tombstone, four Earps are dead and one's in no condition to do anything for months. I hope to hell I'm not here to shoot it out with Doc Holliday."

"Only if you want to," she replied.

"Trust me," said Raven. "I really, truly *don't* want to."

Lisa shrugged. "Well, there you have it."

"Have *what*?" he said, frowning. "Lisa, if I can't come to you for answers, where else can I go?"

"You're preparing for something so vast and complex that there are simply no straightforward or easily comprehensible answers."

Ringo walked over to the table, pulled up a chair from a neighboring table, and sat down.

"Hi, Kate," he said.

"Hello, John," she said coldly.

"Doing well, I trust?"

"Getting by."

"And your boyfriend?"

"Same as always."

"That unpleasant?"

Lisa stood up. "I don't have to listen to this."

She had walked halfway to the door when a familiar voice rang out in the street.

"John Ringo, come out of there, you backstabbing coward!"

Ringo smiled. "The boyfriend," he said, getting to his feet. He walked over to Lisa, took her by the arm despite her flinching from his touch, and led her back to the table. "You'll be safer here," he said.

Then he walked back to the door, looked outside to make

sure Holliday wasn't already covering him with his pistol, and walked out into the street.

"I'm sorry," Raven whispered to Lisa as he got to his feet, "but I've got to see what happens."

He walked to the door, took one step outside, raised his empty hands in the air when Holliday glared at him, and stayed in the shadow of the building.

"John Ringo," growled Holliday, "you killed the only friend I ever had."

Raven resisted the urge to blurt out, "No, it was me!"

"He never really liked you, Doc," said Ringo. "Hell, nobody does. And I'm here to put you out of your misery."

The two men stared at each other, absolutely motionless, for almost ten seconds. Then, by some unseen, unknowable mutual consent, they went for their weapons.

The two shots were fired simultaneously. Onlookers later claimed to have heard only a single shot. Both men flew backward and lay motionless on the ground.

Raven rushed over and looked at the bodies. Holliday had a bloody hole over his heart, and Ringo had a small hole right between his eyes.

"My God, they were as good as everyone thought they were!" he muttered as Lisa joined him.

"I know," she said. "Now come with me."

"But someone has to be an eyewitness for the authorities," protested Raven.

"You and Ringo brought the authorities into town in the back of your wagon," she noted. She pulled gently at his arm. "Now come with me."

He turned reluctantly from the bodies and fell into step beside her.

They turned off the main street, walked over to a totally nondescript street, walked half a block, and then she led him into a small building, abandoned store or bar, he couldn't tell which.

And one step into it she was Lisa again, and then Eddie Raven found himself alone, staring at the walls of his Manhattan apartment.

25

"Damn!" he muttered. "That felt *real*!"

He walked to the refrigerator, opened it, pulled out a can of beer, popped it open, walked into his living room, and sat down on his padded easy chair, trying to assimilate everything that he'd experienced in Tombstone.

There was a knock at the door. He was about to get up when he heard Lisa's voice.

"Stay where you are. I let myself in."

"How did you do that?" he asked. "It was double-locked."

"I am not without my skills," she answered.

She walked into the living room, dressed like the twenty-first-century Lisa once again, stared at him, and then smiled. "I must say that you don't look any the worse for wear."

"What wear?" he said. "We took another imaginary trip, saw a bunch of historical figures shoot it out like on a movie set or maybe Disneyland, and came back."

She smiled. "I heard you say that it felt real."

"Well, it did."

"Of course it did. It *was* real, Eddie."

"Sure," he said sardonically. "I've just been in a gunfight in Tombstone half an hour ago."

"No," she said. "Closer to a century and a half ago."

"Come on," he said irritably. "It was all an illusion. You're the Mistress of Illusions, remember?"

"You really think it was an illusion?" she asked, amused.

"Yes."

"Have you got a computer here?"

"On the desk in the corner," said Raven.

"Do me a favor, Eddie," said Lisa. "Walk over to it and activate it."

He stared at her for a moment, trying to figure out what she was driving at, but finally shrugged, walked over to the desk, seated himself, and activated the computer.

"It's working?" she asked.

He stared at the screen. "It's working."

"Good," she said. "Now Google 'Gunfight at the O.K. Corral.'"

He did as she requested—and was told that no such thing existed.

"Something's wrong with this," he said. "Google can't seem to find it."

"Anything's possible," she said with a shrug. "Can you try to bring up one other thing?"

"What?" asked Raven.

"Gunfight at the Clanton Ranch."

"There's no such thing," said Raven. "It was exciting, but it was imaginary."

"Humor me," she said.

"What the hell," he said with a shrug, typing it in. The screen changed, and he stared at it in rapt fascination.

"Well?" asked Lisa.

"The Gunfight at the Clanton Ranch," he read, "perhaps the

most famous battle of the Old West, took place between two families of the Tombstone, Arizona area—the Earps and the Clantons. When the dust had cleared, four Earps lay dead on the ground. It is thought, though not known for sure, that the notorious gunfighter Johnny Ringo took part in the battle on the Clantons' side."

"Still think it was imaginary?" she asked.

"Let me check a public computer and see if I get the same results, just in case you rigged this one."

"Be my guest."

"Next time we go out."

"Do you really think it'll read any differently?" she asked.

He paused for a long moment, letting what he'd just read sink in. "No, it *really* happened," he said at last. Suddenly he frowned. "And that means that *I* killed Wyatt Earp!"

"You're a better shot than you thought," said Lisa.

"Have I changed any other parts of history?" he asked.

"A few," she said. "A lot of your excursions were to fantasy worlds, where history doesn't exist and hence can't be changed." She smiled. "There are still Munchkins, there's still a Dracula . . ."

"I get the picture," said Raven.

"I hope so, because you've only got one test left."

"Before what?" he asked promptly.

"Before the mission you were created and chosen for," said Lisa.

26

"What test, and what mission?" demanded Raven.

"All will be made clear in the fullness of time," answered Lisa.

"From what you tell me, I haven't *got* the fullness of time," growled Raven.

"Try not to be mad at me, Eddie," she said, reaching out and holding his hand. "I'm not the enemy. In fact, I'm your biggest supporter."

"Then tell me what this final test you mentioned is all about."

She offered him a wan smile and a shrug. "I can't."

"You mean you won't."

She shook her head. "I mean I can't."

"Oh, come on," said Raven irritably. "You knew every other test or adventure or fantasy or call 'em whatever you will in advance, so why not this one?"

"Because your final challenge is beyond my power to create, or even to help you overcome the challenges."

"I've been Dracula and Robin Hood and a Munchkin and Humphrey Bogart and Mordred and Alan Quatermain," said Raven irritably. "How the hell much stranger can it get?"

"It's not a matter of strange, Eddie," said Lisa. "It's a matter of *dangerous*."

"So where does this final test take place, here or in some fantasy world?"

"I don't know," she admitted. "And they weren't fantasy worlds when you were in them."

"You *are* coming along with me, aren't you?" he asked, suddenly suspicious.

"I've taken you as far as I can," she answered. "The final challenge is beyond my scope and power."

"So you won't be there with me?"

She shrugged helplessly. "I don't know."

"Am I never to see you again?" asked Raven suddenly. "Because if that's the case, to hell with everything else, and I'll stay here with you."

"You would not be the man I love if you could turn your back on a universe that is in dire need of you," answered Lisa. "You *must* go through with it."

"Then come with me," he persisted.

She stared at him for a long moment. "Perhaps," she said at last.

"Perhaps?" he repeated. "What the hell does that mean?"

"It means," she replied, "that even the Mistress of Illusions is not totally in control of her own destiny."

"Who *is*?"

She smiled bitterly. "*You* are, of course."

"I'd ask you to explain that," said Raven, "but even if you could I probably wouldn't believe or understand it anyway."

She sighed deeply. "I don't know what else I can say to you."

"How about your devilish friend?"

She frowned. "You mean Rofocale?"

"Yeah," he replied. "You're a local girl I fell for, and he's a guy who got shot by mistake in a holdup." He grimaced. "Or so I thought. But it turned out that you're the Mistress of Illusions and he's the chief demon in Hell. That's a hell of a combo."

"You make us sound so evil, Eddie," she said in hurt tones. "We're trying to *save* the universe, not destroy it."

"I thought *I* was supposed to save it."

"You are," she replied. "But you need preparation. We've been giving it to you."

"Someday you must tell me how being Dracula helped save all of creation," said Raven.

"You learn different approaches with every incarnation, every adventure. We don't know which ones you'll need; we just know that the better prepared you are, the more such approaches you master, the better equipped you will be for whatever you encounter in the Ultimate Challenge."

"Damn!" muttered Raven. "That sounds like it has capital letters in front of each word."

"How perceptive you are," said a familiar voice, and Raven turned to see Rofocale seated on his couch at the other end of the room.

"I'd ask how you got here," said Raven, "but you'd probably tell me, and I've stockpiled enough nightmares already."

Rofocale uttered a single hearty laugh, then sat perfectly still, staring at Raven.

"So are *you* prepared to tell me what the hell this final test is all about?" demanded Raven.

"Certainly," said Rofocale. "It is a test to bring forth and hone those skills that you may need during what the Mistress of Illusions has properly labeled your Ultimate Challenge."

Raven grimaced. "Hell, you're even vaguer than *she* was, and that's going some." He stared at the demon. "This is *my* life we're talking about."

"Your life, and *our* future," replied Rofocale.

"And the future of every living thing anywhere in the universe," added Lisa.

"Well, I'm sure glad it's nothing more important than that," said Raven bitterly. "I'd hate to take the Ultimate Challenge feeling burdened or oppressed in any way."

"Good!" said Rofocale.

"Subtlety's not one of your long and strong points, is it?" asked Raven.

"We all want the same thing, Eddie," said Lisa. "Every single living thing wants it." She sighed. "The problem is, only you can give it to us. I wish it were otherwise—"

"You and me both," Raven cut in.

"But it's not," she concluded. "For what it's worth, you were chosen because you are the one man—the one being—in the universe who can pull it off."

"If I'm *that* awesome," said Raven, "why do I need a final test?"

"Because the opposition is every bit as awesome, and has been preparing its defenses for eons," answered Rofocale.

"Who *is* the opposition?"

"Master the final test and you'll find out soon enough," said the demon. "No sense burdening you with such knowledge now, before we know you'll survive to meet the opposition."

"I admire your notion of confidence-building," said Raven wryly.

"You already know that you are the one entity out of trillions, quadrillions, who *might* be able to emerge triumphant."

Raven grimaced. "Somehow I bet that reads a hell of a lot better than it sounds." He paused. "Do I get to carry any weapons with me?"

"Just your most powerful," said Rofocale.

Raven stared at him curiously.

"The one you were born with, Eddie," said Lisa. "Your brain, your creativity, your willpower—*yourself*."

"Do I have any armor, or shields, or any defenses?"

"Same answer," said Lisa. "Just what you were born with."

"Okay," said Raven. "I assume whatever test I'm facing, I don't take it right here in my apartment. Where do I take it, and how do I get there?"

"Don't worry about it," said Rofocale. "When the time comes, you'll be transported there."

"By plane? Train?" Raven paused. "Horseback?"

Rofocale grinned. "Don't concern yourself with details. One instant you'll be here, the next you won't be."

"Fine. Where *will* I be?"

"Elsewhere," said the demon.

Raven stared at him. "Are you sure we're on the same side?" he said.

"Every living thing on this planet is on your side," said Rofocale.

"Both those who know it and those who don't," added Lisa.

"Am I being transported in the next ten minutes?"

"I really don't know," answered Rofocale.

"If not, there's a great bartender in an all-night tavern over on the next block," said Raven. "I'm going to walk over there for one of his Manhattans while I think about this."

"There's nothing to think about, Eddie," said Lisa. "When the time comes, *poof!*—you're gone."

"Alone?"

She shrugged. "I don't know. No hero, or savior, or call it what you will, has ever done this before." Suddenly she frowned. "At least, none has ever returned from it."

Raven walked to the door. "I assume whoever or whatever it is can find me even if I'm at the bar, or walking to or from it."

"I'll come with you," said Lisa, walking over and joining him.

"Not me," said Rofocale. "I attract too many stares—and this time of night, with no disguise, too damned many of them are hostile."

"Try not to steal my high school track medals," said Raven as he walked out onto the landing, waited for Lisa, and closed and locked the door behind him.

They went down the single flight of stairs, out the front door, and began walking down the sidewalk. Suddenly Raven stopped and stared at her under a streetlamp.

"What is it, Eddie?"

"You know," he said, "I never thought to ask, but is this Lisa I've been seeing and dating all these months really you?"

She nodded her head. "Yes, it is, Eddie," she answered. "Mostly."

"Mostly?" he asked.

"I had a life—quite a long and complex one—before I met

you," said Lisa. "I will probably have another—or the same one, extended—after you accomplish your goals. For the here and now, I'm Lisa and I live in New York."

"Not exactly a definitive answer," remarked Raven.

"I'm sorry," she answered. "But it's as definitive as I can be."

"Somehow I foresaw that answer," he said unhappily. He looked ahead. "Oh, well—we're almost there. And in retrospect, it's just as well Rofocale didn't come along. You never know how late-night drinkers will react to something like him." He grimaced. "Hell, none of 'em have ever even seen something like him."

"He can look a little less awesome when he's in public," she said. "I mean, you saw him at Mako's before the shooting and didn't pay much attention to him."

"True enough," he admitted. "It's just that everything seems a little strange to me these days—except for the things that are *very* strange."

They reached the tavern. He opened the door and stepped aside while she entered, heard a couple of cars crash a block away, tried to spot them, couldn't, and then walked through the doorway.

And found himself *elsewhere*.

27

There was a moment of dizziness and total darkness. When Raven opened his eyes, nothing made any sense.

Buildings were built top-first into the ground, widening as they grew taller. Shapes and colors were all wrong. Running water was alternately green and brown, but always opaque. Same with glass windows. And things that *should* have been opaque, like the walls around public bathrooms and jail cells, were totally transparent.

He heard a growl off to his left and turned to see the source of it. It was a carnivorous dinosaur—an allosaurus if he remembered his textbooks properly—with foot-long teeth. He stared at it, wondering if it meant to charge, and the moment their eyes met it turned and raced away, screeching in terror.

He was just about to relax when a pigeon leveled off and flew at him, clearly intent on plucking out one of his eyeballs. He slapped at it when it got within reach, and it flew away, shrieking in pain or terror or both.

"Lisa?" he said aloud.

There was no answer.

It's a weird venue, he thought, *but if all I have to do is stay alive for however long I'm stuck here, somehow I don't think the universe is in as much trouble as you and Rofocale make it sound.*

"Well, there's no sense standing out here in the open as a target," he muttered. "I think I'd better find someplace that's a little harder to find and easier to defend."

He began walking down the street. An opaque puddle rose up, took on the shape of a ravenously hungry and fang-filled mouth, and tried to take a bite out of him. He ducked and sidestepped, picked up a glowing rock from the street, and hurled it at the puddle, which screamed in agony and flew apart into a hundred pieces, each piece whimpering in terror.

"Watch it, fella," said a stentorian voice behind him. "Even puddles have feelings."

"Who said that?" demanded Raven, spinning around—and finding himself face-to-face with a huge purple-maned lion.

"Who do you think?" growled the lion.

"The damned thing was going to attack me."

"Of course he was. It's his nature."

"Well, *my* nature is to defend myself," said Raven.

"And mine is to kill and eat anything weaker than myself."

Think, Eddie, Lisa's voice seemed to say.

"Then it's a good thing I'm stronger than you," said Raven.

The lion swallowed hard. "You are?"

"Want a demonstration?" said Raven. "I can't promise you'll live through it, but that's hardly *my* problem."

Suddenly the lion began shrinking until it was the size of a housecat. "You wouldn't hurt a little guy like me, would you?" he whined.

"Not if he gets out of my sight, and is quick about it," replied Raven.

The cat raced off between two hideously misshapen buildings.

Is that the best the world's got to offer? thought Raven. *Cowardly cats and dinosaurs?*

No, Eddie, answered Lisa. *I wish it were, but you're on the very outskirts. Believe me, you're going to need all your courage and skills before you're through.*

I can't tell you how encouraging that is, thought Raven wryly. *Are you in this venue too?*

No, not yet, she replied. *Maybe not ever. It all depends.*

On what?

On you, of course.

And suddenly he sensed that they were no longer in contact.

He decided that until he found a reliable form of transportation he'd better hunt up what they would call in spy novels and movies a safe house, a place where he could relax, consider his next move, and replenish his mental and physical energy.

He looked up and down the street and ruled out all one-story buildings. Sooner or later there had to be another dinosaur or something similar, but with a temper, and a creature like that could tear such a dwelling apart with almost no effort.

By the same token, he didn't want anything too high. The way this world worked—or, rather, *didn't* work—he could climb to the fifth or tenth or thirtieth floor, only to find that the stairs or elevator had vanished once he got there . . . or worse still, *while* he was getting there.

He began walking, passing one unacceptable building after another. After two blocks the street swerved and spent about fifty yards winding around the base of a mountain that, as far as Raven could tell, had no geologic reason for being there. As he began walking down the street, which became a twisty path through the mountain, he passed a small cave on his left.

He stopped, faced it, and called, "Anyone there?"

"Damned right there is!" growled a very strange-sounding voice, and a moment later a creature that had clearly never existed on Earth emerged and confronted him.

The being was perhaps seven feet tall, and at least that wide. Its flesh looked like it was formed of rock. It seemed to have one leg when it stood still, but when it stepped forward the one leg split into two, then rejoined when it stood still again.

"Friend or enemy?" asked Raven.

"Yes," was the reply.

"You got a name?"

"Of course I have a name," answered the creature. "Everyone has a name."

"What is it?" asked Raven.

The creature frowned. "Damn!" it growled. "I hate questions like that."

"Why don't I just call you Stranger?" suggested Raven. "After all, you're stranger than just about everything else I've encountered here."

"Stranger . . . Stranger . . ." muttered the creature. Suddenly it shot him a toothy grin. "I *like* it!"

"Okay, Stranger," said Raven. "How do I get out of here?"

"Which way did you come in?"

Raven shrugged. "I don't know."

"Well, that *does* make it harder." Stranger frowned. "I suppose we could walk to the horizon and see if we fall off."

"Off a *world*, with gravity and the like?" said Raven, frowning.

"Do you know for a fact this is a world?" demanded Stranger. "Maybe it's just a mildly flat piece of cosmic debris."

"No, it's a world," said Raven. "It's got gravity, and some kind of almost comprehensible ecosystem."

"Okay, it's a world. Why do you want to get off it?"

"It's not *my* world."

"It's not mine either," replied Stranger. "But I find lots to eat, and so far hardly anything has attacked me, and I like the gravity, and I can breathe what passes for the air, and—"

Raven shook his head. "I want *my* world."

"Well then, we might as well go looking for it," said Stranger. "Round, was it?"

"Pretty much so."

"Blue?"

"The oceans, yeah."

"The oceans, not the continents?" asked Stranger.

"Right."

The creature shook its head in wonderment. "Very odd world." He paused. "Got air?"

"Couldn't breathe if it didn't," said Raven.

"You'd be surprised what people can breathe when they have to," said Stranger.

Raven grimaced. "Yeah, I have a horrible feeling that I would be."

"Okay," said Stranger. "Let's get started."

"Which way?"

Stranger frowned. "Beats the hell out of me." He looked around, then pointed off to his left. "I've never been that way before. Been most other directions, and I'm still here."

"Let's go," said Raven, walking off.

Stranger joined him, and they walked across a rough, rocky landscape for close to a mile.

"Be careful," warned Raven. "It's so dark I can't see the ground, and that means I can't see any bumps or holes or even small carnivores."

"Makes no difference," replied Stranger. "After all, ground is"—there was a sudden surprised gasp—"grouuuund."

Raven turned to his companion, only to find that he wasn't there.

"Stranger?" he said.

"Down here!" came the answer from what seemed a quarter mile away.

Raven couldn't see anything, but examined the ground with the toe of his shoe and found a large hole that hadn't been there when he walked over it a few seconds ahead of Stranger.

"Are you all right?" he shouted down the hole. "Anything broken?"

"Of course something's broken!" snapped Stranger. "The ground where I was walking."

"Nothing broken on your body, though?"

"I don't think so," said Stranger. "But I've never broken anything before—well, except a tooth—so how would I know?"

Raven peered into the pit, but it was too dark to see his companion.

"How the hell are we going to get you out of there?" he said.

"I don't know," answered Stranger. "I suppose you need the

longest rope in existence, or one hell of an impressive set or stairs, or—" The voice went still for a moment. "Well, how about that?" it continued in a happier tone.

"What happened?" asked Raven.

"A wall opened, and a dim light went on in an adjacent chamber, and there's a table with a hell of a spread laid out on it: chimera liver, ogre eyes, and what looks like pickled unicorn horns." Another brief pause. "You go ahead without me. This was my own fault, so I'll stay behind and suffer."

"You sure?"

"Go, goddammit!"

Raven shrugged and turned to once again face the dark, foreboding, not-quite-empty world.

Well, what the hell, I don't suppose it really matters. Might as well keep going in the same direction.

He headed off, and after another mile the sound of laughter came to his ears.

Some final exam, he thought as he turned and headed toward the sound. *The worst things I've encountered so far are a nonaggressive dinosaur, a lion, Stranger, and a hole in the ground.*

He heard a loud hissing noise off to his left, turned to face it, and found that it was either a very large worm or a very small snake. He ignored it and kept walking.

He'd gone about two hundred yards when he heard a soft, delicate meow. Thinking a small cat or a kitten might make a nice traveling companion, especially if it could see in the dark, he paused and faced the gentle meowing.

"Join me," he said softly. "I won't hurt you."

Another meow, just the slightest bit louder.

"Here, boy—or girl," he said in gentle tones.

Then came a meow that was literally next to him, and he felt a huge expulsion of foul-smelling breath. He looked up, and found himself facing a feline creature about the size of a bull elephant, with fangs almost as long as his arms.

"Forget I mentioned it," said Raven, backing away.

The creature approached him.

"Scram," he said in his softest, least aggressive tone.

The creature reached out a tongue and licked his arm—and the sleeve came away on its tongue. It made a face, spit out the cloth, and emitted an ear-shattering roar.

Raven would have run, but he couldn't see more than fifty feet in any direction, and besides he was certain there was no way he could outrun a pachyderm-size cat, so he stared at the creature for a minute and then yelled, "Get the hell out of my way!"

It jumped back a few feet, stared at him, and growled, which sounded to Raven not unlike a volcano about to explode.

"Beat it!" screamed Raven, and the creature jumped back again.

Raven reached down, picked up a rock, and hurled it at the creature's nose as hard as he could.

The creature moved slightly, caught it in its mouth, chewed it with a loud crunching noise, made a sound that Raven couldn't interpret, turned, and walked away.

Raven stared after it for a long moment, then shrugged, and recommenced walking. After half an hour he saw a very strange structure about half a mile ahead. As he got closer, he saw that it was a single manufactured creation, though unlike any he had ever seen. It was vaguely hexagonal in structure, but there were literally hundreds of departures from that design, and the building materials seemed to change every few feet—and in some cases every few inches.

From where he stood he couldn't tell if the walls surrounded an empty space a hundred or more yards across, or if the walls contained a totally solid structure. He looked for a light, listened for a sound, remained alert for any sign that the structure was inhabited—and finally he heard the faintest strain of music from a harplike instrument.

He began walking along the building's wall, certain there must be an entrance *some*where. He didn't fully trust his eyes, so he reached an arm out and slid it along the wall as he walked—and indeed, after about one hundred yards he came to an indentation. He stopped, couldn't see it even from two feet away, but used his hands to determine its outline, which was about three feet wide and somewhat higher than he could reach.

I could wander out here forever, he thought, *and what would it prove? Where would it get me? I'm trying to get back to my world, and maybe there's someone in there who can help. Of course, no one's helped yet, but no one's misled me or done me any harm, so what the hell.*

He felt for a doorknob or handle but couldn't find one. He was prepared to ram his shoulder against the portal and shove, but when he thought about it, realized that this world had constantly surprised him, and pushed gently against the door—and, of course, almost the second he made contact with it, it vanished.

He stepped through and found himself in what seemed to

be a covered, dimly lit courtyard. Parts were lit by flaming torches, parts by laser beams.

"You there!" cried out a deep, stentorian voice. "Halt!"

"You speak English," replied Raven, frowning. "Are we somehow on Earth? I mean, where the hell else would they speak it?"

"Earth?" said the voice, and Raven saw that it came from a mildly human figure with three eyes, a nose on each cheek, an ear where his nose should have been, and a robe that kept changing from primary to pastel colors and back again. A golden dagger resided in a sheath wrapped around its waist. "Where is Earth?"

Raven shrugged. "Beats the hell out of me. I'm trying to find it."

"Must be an interesting place if you're typical of it," said the robed figure. "You're physically as close to one of the People as anyone who's yet made his way to the Holy Land here." Suddenly he frowned. "Why are you here?"

"I'm lost," answered Raven.

"You *do* know the penalty for invading the Holy Land?"

"Of course not," said Raven irritably. "I just got here. Let me leave and we can part friends, a quantity I suspect you do not possess in abundance."

"It's a novel thought," admitted the robed figure. "But once you're beyond the wall you're in Inferno, so why do I need a friend there?"

"Have none of you ever been outside the wall?" asked Raven.

"Certainly not."

"You've been misinformed."

"Blasphemy!" cried the robed figure, and suddenly he was joined by ten more similarly garbed figures.

"If it's blasphemy, how come I'm standing here, safe and sound, having just walked in from your mistaken notion of Inferno?"

"You know," said another of the beings, "he *is* the second one to claim to be from Inferno. Maybe there's something to it."

"They could all live there, waiting to overcome us," said the robed figure. "After all, they *are* the same race."

"You have someone else of my race here?" asked Raven.

"I just said so."

"May I see him? If he knows how to get back to where we came from, the pair of us can take our leave of you and no one will be any the worse for it."

"I shall have to think upon it," said the robed figure.

Raven stared at him. "Try not to take too long," he said. "If I get hungry, I may eat you . . . and if I get restless, I may tear apart your Holy Land."

He stood absolutely still, studying their faces to see if he'd said it forcefully enough so that a few of them at least believed it.

Finally the leader spoke. "All right," he said. "Bring the other one."

Half a dozen of his warriors went off behind a structure, and Raven lost sight of them. They returned a few minutes later, half of them pulling a lovely silk-clad girl by her bonds, the other half prodding her from behind with their spears.

Raven watched the procession until she was close enough for him to make out her features.

"Lisa!" he exclaimed.

"Hello, Eddie," she answered.

"What the hell are *you* doing here?"

"I told you it was possible that I'd wind up in part of your mission," said Lisa. She frowned. "I just never guessed it would be *this* part."

"You know each other," stated the leader. It was not a question.

"Yes," said Raven. "Now release her and we'll be on our way."

"Why should I take your word for it?" demanded the leader.

"Because you have nothing to gain by holding her," replied Raven.

"How do you know?" scoffed the leader.

Raven reached the leader in three quick steps, pulled the creature's gold-handled dagger out of its sheath, stood behind him, wrapped an arm around him, and held the blade to his throat.

"It's up to you, of course," said Raven, "but my guess is that what you have to gain by releasing her is your life."

Half a dozen warriors withdrew their swords and began approaching the pair.

"No!" cried the leader. "Let him go!" The beings who were approaching suddenly stopped. "The creature has a point. I'll live a lot longer if you all back away and I allow him to escape with the female unmolested."

The creatures backed away, leaving a path for Raven and Lisa to a nearby wall, which became translucent, then transparent, and finally nonexistent as they approached it.

"How long were you there?" asked Raven when they were outside and the wall had solidified behind them.

Lisa shrugged. "I don't know. It seems we were just talking in that bar an hour or two ago, but time doesn't have much meaning in this universe."

"Are you all right?"

"They didn't torture or mistreat me, if that's what you mean," she replied. "But it feels as if I've been in that damned dungeon for weeks." Suddenly she shrugged. "Hell, for all I know, I *have* been. Like I say, time is very subjective in this venue."

"Well, we might as well start looking for a way home," said Raven. "At least I managed to rescue you and escape from that crazy place. I assume *that* was my test."

She shook her head. "No, Eddie."

"No?"

"It was too easy," said Lisa. "Just kind of a first step."

Raven frowned. "You're sure?"

She nodded her head. "I'm sure."

"But you've never been here before—so how can you *know*?"

"Because, Eddie," she said seriously, "you are not the first candidate. In point of fact, you are the fifth since the human race was established—and none of the first four ever returned. They were skilled, resourceful men, as you are. It *has* to be more difficult."

"All four are dead?"

She shrugged. "We've no idea, though we assume so. All we know for sure is that they're gone."

Raven frowned. "Okay, I guess we're stuck here a little longer." He reached out and held her hand. "At least we're together. We might as well find the equivalent of a safe house where we can get a little rest."

She smiled bitterly. "On *this* world, in *this* universe?"

"Unless you plan to rest somewhere else," he said. "It's been a long day."

She made no reply, and they began walking. Soon the wall vanished, though it was so dark they could only tell it was gone by the fact that they could no longer feel it. They continued, came to a small, misshapen building, couldn't find a door or any other method of entering it, and proceeded again.

"Worse comes to worst, we'll take turns napping and standing guard over each other," said Raven. "But I can't believe this entire world hasn't got a few hundred shelters, maybe even more."

They heard an inhuman shriek in the distance.

"It certainly seems to need them," added Raven.

They walked around what seemed to be an open plain. As they neared the far edge of it, they could tell they were facing artificial structures, but they couldn't make them out in the near-total darkness. Then, suddenly, a voice chimed out: "Hey, fella—you and the lady need a lift?"

Raven and Lisa froze, trying fruitlessly to spot the speaker.

"Well?" said the voice.

"I can't see you," said Raven.

"Damn, that's right! You're a human, aren't you?"

"Yes."

"Stay where you are," said the voice. "I'll be right over."

Raven thought he could see some movement ahead and to his right, but the more he concentrated the more difficult it became. Finally he relaxed and suddenly he was confronting a creature out of one of his childhood nightmares. It possessed a crocodile's mouth and teeth, a neck as long as a brontosaur's, a body covered with spikes (all pointing outward, of course), and six sturdy legs, each ending in fearsome-looking claws.

"So where are you heading?" asked the creature.

"Home," said Raven.

The creature chuckled and blew thick blue vapor out of its huge nostrils. "Biped, two arms, one head, taller than a squirrel, shorter than a Denebian Sand Devil. I need more info, pal. Home could be any one of seventeen hundred and three worlds."

"Class C star, eight major planets, an asteroid belt between the fourth and fifth planet, and possibly a runaway moon beyond the eighth planet."

"Good," said the creature. "That boils it down to only thirteen." It paused. "By the way, my name's—um, let me think—ah, got it, my name's Jasper."

"You forgot your name?" asked Raven.

"Certainly not. But for an instant there I forgot how to translate it into your primitive, dismal language. And you are?"

"She's Lisa, I'm Eddie," said Raven.

"Well, let's get started," said Jasper. "Name of planet you want to find?"

"Earth."

"And the star?"

"We call it the sun, but officially it's Sol."

"Fine," said Jasper. "Now, which direction is Sol?"

Raven shrugged. "I've no idea."

"Take a guess."

"Up?"

"I need a little more than that."

"I don't know."

"Well, you'd better remember fast," said Jasper. "We're being approached by a carnotaur, and he smells hungry." A brief pause. "Of course, they *all* smell hungry, probably because they all are."

"Can we climb aboard you and trust you to keep out of his way until we can come up with better directions for getting home?" asked Raven.

"It's worth a try," said Jasper, and they became aware of his huge body walking up and coming to a stop right next to them.

"I can outrun any carnotaur that was ever foaled." He paused. "Or are they whelped, or maybe hatched?"

"How do we get onto you?" asked Raven.

"Try the stairs, of course," answered Jasper, and suddenly Raven and Lisa saw a staircase descending from the creature's back, which was about thirty feet above the ground.

"After you," said Raven, standing aside.

"But you're the vital one," complained Lisa.

"Then the sooner you climb onto his back, the sooner I can follow you and the less chance that I'll be eaten or whatever by the carnotaur."

She seemed about to protest, then shrugged and began racing up the stairs. He followed instantly, and a moment later both were perched precariously along Jasper's spine.

"Stop shifting your weight and moving your feet, or you'll fall off," said Jasper. "And the carnotaur is getting closer every second. Well, every second and two-fifths, anyway."

"Your back keeps moving when you walk or run, even when you breathe," replied Raven. "We can't stay up here *without* shifting our weight."

"Oh, my goodness!" said Jasper. "I hadn't thought of that. Here!"

And as the last words were uttered, a pair of comfortable benches composed of Jasper's bone and flesh rose and took shape right behind them.

"Better?" asked Jasper.

"Much," said Lisa.

"Good, because I'm going to have to start a little evasive maneuvering," said Jasper. "The damned carnotaur seems to have brought its whole ugly brood with it. There are five—no, six—of the little bastards. Just a sec!"

Suddenly their benches, and Jasper's back, began bouncing wildly, and they heard a chorus of agonized high-pitched screeches.

"Make that three of the little bastards now," said Jasper. "Mama, or maybe it's Papa, never taught them the basics of hunting anything that could fight back."

"So once we elude the carnotaur . . ." began Raven.

"Wrong tense," said Jasper. "It just gave up the chase."

"Okay," said Raven. "Where do we go now?"

"Well, we're *not* going to try all thirteen worlds without a plan," said Jasper. "Hell, with my luck, your world will be the thirteenth, and two or three of the early ones will have critters that like nothing more than eating sweet, innocent, unassuming, not-quite-hideous beasts like myself."

"I'm open to suggestions," said Raven.

"So am I," replied Jasper. "I'm not quite up there with Mephistopheles or even Houdini, but I intuit that you're here to prove yourself, perhaps to this gorgeous damsel here, so probably I should turn the planning and thinking over to you and just act as transportation."

"Even if due to my inexperience on this world I direct you to certain death?" asked Raven.

"Let me think about that," said Jasper.

"Simple question," said Raven. "What's to think about?"

"I *hate* dying!" exclaimed Jasper. "It's always too messy, and occasionally painful." He paused. "Especially the third time."

"You've died three times?" asked Raven, surprised.

"Five, actually," answered Jasper. "But the third was the worst."

"Strange world," mused Raven softly. "I wonder how many times *I* can die?"

"Once and out," said Lisa. "You're a *man*. Jasper is a . . . well, something else."

"Okay," said Raven. "It makes a depressing kind of sense when you put it that way." He was silent for a moment. "Jasper, take us to this world's exit point. Maybe once we're there I can dope out which planet is Earth."

"That's only part of it," said Jasper.

"Why am I not surprised?" muttered Raven. "What's the other part?"

"*Parts,*" said Jasper. "Plural."

"Okay, shoot."

"I don't have a gun."

"I mean, let me know what the parts are."

"Well, first you want a date, or at least an era," answered Jasper. "From what little I know of oxygen worlds, without that I could drop you off a couple of hundred million years before your own time, in the middle of carnotaur hatching

season. Or I could dump you a few million years in your future, after the atmosphere has turned toxic and everyone has
long since emigrated to more hospitable worlds."

"Okay," said Raven. "What else do you need to know?"

"A location," said Jasper. "Most planets capable of sustain-
ing oxygen-breathing life have polar ice caps. I could drop you
off on one with no protection from the cold—or in the middle
of an ocean, thousands of miles from shore but a lot closer
than that to a school—hell, a whole university—of sharks."

"You sure know how to cheer a guy up," muttered Raven.

"You really think so?" replied Jasper enthusiastically. "Maybe
I missed my calling. Maybe I should have been a nightclub
comedian, once they invent nightclubs on this godforsaken
world."

"Best of luck to you," said Raven unenthusiastically.

"Oh, by the way, hold tight!" said Jasper suddenly.

Raven and Lisa had a sudden sensation of falling, then set-
tled back in their seats as Jasper seemed to be rising again.

"What the hell was *that* all about?" demanded Raven.

"Canyon," explained Jasper. "Only saw it after I'd started
dropping down into it."

"How long until we reach whatever the hell it is you call
our destination?"

"I thought it was Earth," said Jasper, puzzled.

"I mean, our point of departure."

"Oh, anywhere from three minutes to a week, always assuming your week has four days like mine does."

"Why the difference?"

"Depends on whether the Slaughter Machine is patrolling
the area when we get there," answered Jasper.

"The Slaughter Machine?" repeated Raven. "That sounds ominous."

"Only when it's on duty."

"What the hell is it?"

"An entity—"

"Entity?" interrupted Raven.

"I don't know if it's a machine or a living being," explained Jasper. "But it does tend to kill anyone who tries to leave without a ticket or a passport, though in truth I have no idea whether it eats them or simply defenestrates them."

"The Slaughter Machine patrols a lot of such areas, does it?" asked Raven.

"No, just the one we're headed to."

"Then why might it be anywhere else?"

"It probably isn't," answered Jasper.

Raven frowned. "Then let's assume it's here."

"I ran the figures in my head, and there's a point zero zero zero three percent chance that it will be elsewhere. I am a logical entity. I have to take every possibility into account."

"Let's go with the odds," said Raven. "Assume the Slaughter Machine is waiting for us."

Jasper considered it for a moment. "Seems logical," it said at last. "Besides, I *hate* dying."

"You and us both," said Raven.

"The alternative is to stay here for eternity and whatever comes after," said Jasper. "You choose."

"Go to the exit point," said Raven.

Jasper flapped his wings, and Raven and Lisa felt the compression as he rose higher and began attaining more speed.

"Somehow this isn't what I had in mind when I went through that portal," said Raven.

"I'm sure it's different every time," replied Lisa.

"I've been trying to imagine what a Slaughter Machine must be like," remarked Raven. He turned to her. "Whatever the hell it is, just stay clear of it. This isn't *your* final exam."

She stared at him, looked like she wanted to disagree, but made no comment.

They flew in silence for fifteen minutes. Then Raven spoke up. "Are we getting any closer?"

"Of course we are," answered Jasper.

"Any traffic, or are we the only ones?"

"We're the only one on this route to what you call the exit point," said Jasper. "I have no idea if it's being approached from other directions, or if any ships are on the ground there."

"How much longer?" asked Raven.

"About three hundred balumbas," said Jasper.

Raven signed. "And how long is a balumba?"

"You weren't the brightest one in your class, were you?" replied Jasper.

"Just answer the question."

"Maybe forty pirellas."

Raven sighed deeply. "I'm sorry I asked."

"Don't be," said Jasper. "At least you'll die a better-educated corpse when you finally come face-to-whatever with the Slaughter Machine."

"Thanks for the encouragement."

"Freely given," answered Jasper. Then: "Brace yourselves. Coming in for a landing."

"Can't you just hover over the spot you want to land at and then lower yourself to the ground?" asked Raven.

"Son of a grunch!" exclaimed Jasper happily. "I never thought of that!"

Jasper came to a halt in midair, and then very slowly, very gently, lowered himself to a solid surface.

"How was that?" he asked.

"Very comfortable," answered Raven. "Add it to your repertoire."

"I definitely will," said Jasper. "Always assuming we survive the next few minutes."

"Okay," said Raven, getting to his feet. Lisa stood up as well. He knew ordering her to sit back down would be fruitless, and he couldn't bring himself to push her back onto her seat. "Where is it?"

"The Slaughter Machine?" said Jasper. "On the ground, just beyond this door."

The door vanished.

Raven stood in the open doorway and surveyed the area. It was dark, as the rest of the planet had been, but not so dark that he couldn't see a sleek, alien-looking building with a large open doorway some fifty yards away.

Then a movement off to his left caught his attention, and he turned to face the strangest thing he had ever seen. It had sixteen mechanical arms and legs, all of different lengths, all armed, some with blades, some with what seemed like explosive weapons, some that were beyond Raven's ability to identify. It possessed six glowing eyes circling its massive head, and three legs that seemed almost too light and agile to carry that massive armed and armored body.

"Who approaches?" it demanded.

"You speak English," noted Raven.

"I speak directly to your brain," replied the Slaughter Machine, "so language and translation aren't necessary. Now state your purpose for being here."

"This lady"—he indicated Lisa, who was now standing beside him—"and I wish to go home."

"And where is home?"

"Earth, the third planet circling Sol."

"Words!" growled the machine contemptuously. *"Think!"*

Raven tried to picture a celestial map of the solar system, then dwelt on the conversation he'd had with Jasper about Earth's location.

"Ah!" said the Slaughter Machine. "Earth."

"Yes."

"And how do you expect to get there?"

"I'm told we can reach it through the local exit point, which is to say the building behind you."

"Have you the password?"

Raven frowned. "No."

"Have you purchased passage with the necessary combination of the one hundred twentieth through the one hundred twenty-seventh elements?"

"No."

"Then you may not leave."

"Have you a superior I can speak to?" asked Raven.

"Nothing is superior to the Slaughter Machine," was its answer. "Not only may you not leave, but for your impertinence you may not live."

Raven studied the machine. When it spoke he could see

some lights flashing inside it; otherwise it remained as dark and foreboding as when he'd first seen it.

"How do you know *I* won't let *you* live?" said Raven.

"I am not alive, and therefore cannot be killed," said the Slaughter Machine.

"You can't be killed in the sense that I can be," agreed Raven, "but you can be terminated."

"How?" demanded the machine.

"Let's put that powerful brain of yours to work and see," said Raven. He paused for a few seconds. "Ready?"

"I am ready," said the machine.

"Are you never wrong?"

"It is impossible for me to err."

"Okay," said Raven. "I've got an easy one for you to start with. How much are five plus four?"

"Nine, of course."

"You're sure?"

"Absolutely," said the machine.

"No exceptions under any circumstances?"

"None."

"And if we find an exception you've made a mistake?"

"Yes."

"Okay," said Raven. "Compute in Base Seven."

The machine was silent for a moment, then uttered a truly ear-splitting scream. What passed for its head slumped forward, the lighting and whirring of gears it had possessed stopped, and it remained totally motionless.

"I don't understand what just happened, Eddie," said Lisa.

"Simple math. Any high schooler can do it—though I don't think they do these days—and even some grade school kids.

We compute almost everything in Base One. When you use different bases, you sometimes—not always, but often—come up with different answers to the same problems."

"That's remarkable!" she said.

He shot her a self-deprecating smile. "That's the benefit of a high school education."

She looked around. "So what do we do now?"

"Enter the station here and book passage home."

"We didn't exactly fly here," she said.

"I'm sure they know that," he replied, taking her arm and leading her into the building.

They found themselves in a large, empty room. A moment later an incredibly ancient humanoid alien, his skin discolored and wrinkled, approached them.

"Mr. Raven and companion," he said, coming to a stop and staring at them. "The betting was that we'd never see you at this location."

"Then you know what we want," said Raven.

"Of course."

"And?"

"It's quite ready for you." The old man began hobbling off to his right. "Follow me, please."

Raven and Lisa fell into step behind him. They soon reached a totally smooth, featureless wall. The old man ran his hand across a small section of it, and suddenly a door appeared.

"Have a safe trip," he said.

Raven took hold of Lisa's hand, and together they walked through the doorway—

28

—A nd found themselves in Raven's living room.

"Sonofabitch!" he exclaimed. "We're back!"

"Yes, we are, Eddie," said Lisa.

"And even more startling, we're still alive!"

"That's because you used your skills," she said.

"There were moments when I didn't think we were going to make it." He paused and stared at her. "Where the hell were we?"

She shrugged. "Elsewhere."

"Let's just hope to hell we never have to go back."

"We won't."

"You're sure?" he asked.

"You've beaten that world, Eddie. Now you're as fully prepared for the Final Confrontation as you'll ever be."

"If I beat that world," he said, staring at her, "it's because I couldn't leave you there." Suddenly he smiled. "I think I deserve a prize for surviving it."

"A prize?"

He nodded his head. "Right."

"What kind of prize?" asked Lisa.

He stared into her eyes. "A wife."

"I'm flattered," she said.

"I love you, Lisa. I think I've loved you from the day we met."

"I love you too, Eddie," she replied. "But there's a universe to be saved." Suddenly she grimaced. "And if you don't save it, neither we nor the world we know will be around long enough for the wedding."

"I've read a lot of science fiction books about one man or one woman saving all of Creation," replied Raven. "Maybe I can learn something from them."

"You can try," she said dubiously. "But I doubt it."

"Oh?" he replied. "Why?"

"If they're like most of the science fiction books I've seen on the stands or in the stores, they're about one man, or one small group of men, fighting off military forces or reversing scientific cataclysms." She smiled sadly. "Our universe isn't under that kind of threat."

"What kind *are* we under?" asked Raven.

"I think I'll let Rofocale explain it to you," said Lisa. "I get too emotional just thinking about a sudden end to it."

"To it?" he repeated.

"To all of existence," she said.

He made a face, then shrugged. "Okay, so maybe it's not like the typical science fiction book, but really, how the hell different can it be?"

"It's not only that, Eddie," she replied. "It's you, too."

"How so?"

"You have very special skills, Eddie," said Lisa. "A tiny handful of others may have had them in the past, but only you have mastered them to the fullest extent."

"What about the four men who went ahead of me?" asked Raven.

She shook her head. "They didn't have your abilities, Eddie."

"You didn't know them," said Raven. "At least, I assume you didn't." *At least, you'd better not have, since I assume they existed centuries or possibly even millennia ago.* "So how could you possibly know that?"

"Because they had everything going for them," answered Lisa. "They had advantages that you are lacking—and they are all dead, while you have survived."

Suddenly Raven started feeling restless and constricted. "It's warm and stuffy in here," he said. "Care to go for a walk, and maybe grab some dinner, or breakfast, or whatever the hell it's time for?"

"Why not?" she said with a shrug. She walked to the door, then stepped aside as he opened it for her.

It was a pleasant night, and both of them felt relaxed after the ordeal they had undergone. Raven headed toward Mako's shop, and was surprised to see an Out of Business sign taped to a window, right next to a For Rent sign.

"You look puzzled, Eddie," remarked Lisa.

"I just wanted to see it one more time, since it's where everything started," he said. "I'm surprised mere physical force could run a supernatural shop like this out of business."

"The shop wasn't supernatural," Lisa replied. "Neither were Mako or his customers, as you well know. A few of the sales items were, but they were created elsewhere and elsewhen, then shipped here to be displayed."

"Still," said Raven, looking at the freshly replaced walls and windows, "this is where it all started. It should have *something* a little extraordinary about it."

"Be grateful that it doesn't, or it might still be attracting our enemies."

"Your and Rofocale's enemies," replied Raven with a humorless smile.

"Who do you think you've been fighting for the past few weeks, Eddie?" said Lisa.

"Point taken," he conceded. He stared into the shop for another few second. "Ah, well, there's nothing else to see here. Ready for some dinner?"

"Sounds good," replied Lisa.

"I agree," said a familiar voice. "I'm famished."

Raven looked to his left and saw that Rofocale had joined them.

"So we're all one big happy family now?" he said.

Rofocale smiled at him. "Briefly," he said as the smile vanished.

29

Raven frowned as the waiter seated them at a corner table and disappeared into the depths of the kitchen.

"What's the matter, Eddie?" asked Lisa.

"I don't understand," said Raven.

"What don't you understand?"

"Look at Rofocale. He's built like a pair of Mr. Americas pushed together. He's a brighter red than any fire truck you ever saw. He's got pointed ears. He's got to be over seven feet tall. And no one is looking at him—not the waiter, not the bartender, not even that couple two tables away."

"They see what I want them to see," said Rofocale. "You and the entity you know as Lisa see me as I really am."

"She *is* Lisa," insisted Raven.

Rofocale turned to Lisa with a smile. "Are you Lisa?"

"To Eddie I am," she replied. "That's all that matters."

"Says the Mistress of Illusions," added Rofocale. He smiled. "We are *all* very special creatures."

Raven shook his head. "I'm nothing special. I'm certainly no hero. I didn't win a duel to the death or anything like that. I used an old math trick that almost no one in the world cares about. I'm just a guy from Manhattan."

"You are much more than that, Eddie," said Rofocale.

"I don't destroy bad guys," insisted Raven. "I sell dresses."

"A masterful disguise."

"It's no disguise, damn it!" snapped Raven. "It's *me*!"

Lisa shook her head. "No, Eddie," she said. "You must know by now that you are far more than that, far more than you can currently imagine or comprehend, or you would not have been chosen for the Final Confrontation."

"Half of me wants to believe you, and the other half thinks I'll be joining you two at the funny farm if I buy into it. I'm just Eddie Raven, damn it, and if I ever do anything of note it'll be coming up with some knock-off that outsells Oscar de la Renta or Miuccia Prada knock-offs."

Rofocale chuckled deep in his massive throat. "You have far more potential than that—and the sooner you understand it the better, because the Master of Dreams, whom you defeated at the start of this ongoing adventure, and the world you just returned from were merely stalking horses for a far worse enemy who awaits you, who indeed awaits all of us if you cannot stop him. *That* is the one you must defeat if anyone on Earth or any other planet, not just in the solar system or the galaxy, but in the universe, is to survive."

"To hell with it—and you!" growled Raven. "I've had it with Masters of Dreams and fantasy worlds and having the girl I love used for target practice."

"It's not as if you have a choice," said Rofocale. "This is what you were born—*created*—for, Eddie."

Lisa reached over and laid her hand on Raven's. "You would not be the man I love if you could turn your back on a universe that is in such dire need of you. You *must* face this challenge, wherever it may lead you."

"You must understand, Eddie," said Rofocale, "that all ambiguity ends right here and right now."

"Explain!" demanded Raven.

"What you must face and defeat if any living thing is to survive anywhere in the universe is the ultimate, unambiguous manifestation of evil incarnate—the Lord of Nightmares. All things, favorable and otherwise, follow from that."

"The Lord of Nightmares?" repeated Raven. "It sounds like a bad joke."

"Are we smiling?" asked Rofocale, and suddenly both he and Lisa faded into nothingness.

"And," said Rofocale's disembodied voice, becoming softer with each word, "you must defeat him on your own."

And suddenly Eddie Raven was left alone with his memories, his challenges, and his doubts.